THE SHIMMERING
──── BOOK 1 ────

The Shimmering

MICHAEL L. CLARK

Published by Historic Traces Publishing

Pensacola, Florida 32534

ISBN: 979-8-9887856-4-4 (Paperback)

ISBN: 979-8-9887856-5-1 (Hardback)

ISBN: 979-8-9887856-6-8 (Digital)

To my wife, Cindy, and my daughters, Casey and Savannah, who have encouraged me to always follow my dreams.

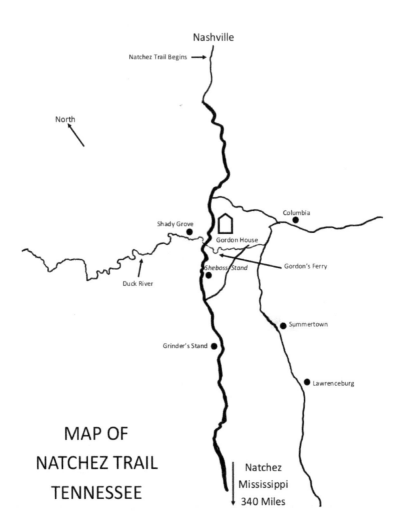

Nashville

Natchez Trail Begins ➔

North

Shady Grove ●

Columbia ●

Gordon House

Sheboss Stand ●

Gordon's Ferry

Duck River

Summertown ●

Grinder's Stand ●

Lawrenceburg ●

MAP OF
NATCHEZ TRAIL
TENNESSEE

Natchez
Mississippi
340 Miles

PROLOGUE

June 21, 1973: It was 7:00 a.m. when the 1964 VW bus turned off Highway 20 onto the Natchez Trace Parkway. Two young men traveled together on their short quest to find herbs and plants useful to the family. They left the Grove earlier that morning, being instructed by one of the elders to find the needed items to supplement the crops grown in their community. The Grove was a community of people with similar ideals that had moved into the area in 1971. The locals around Summertown, Tennessee, called them hippies. They had moved into the area from the San Francisco area, searching for affordable land where they could live together in peace. They were people who preached against violence but were not against the use of certain hallucinogenic plants to enhance their self-awareness.

Robbie and August were the happy young men selected for this special quest. Robbie was eighteen years old. He wore his long, stringy hair pulled back into a ponytail. He had a little thin mustache on his upper lip that was barely visible to the human eye. He wore bell-bottom jeans and a T-shirt with Haight-Ashbury printed on the front. August was sixteen. His long blond hair was left free and flowing down his back. He had pale blue eyes, and his little pug nose turned up a little at the end. He, too, wore bell-bottom jeans, but his T-shirt of choice was tie-dyed.

The two young men traveled down the parkway at a leisurely pace. Their transistor radio, hanging from the bus's rearview mirror, was blaring an FM station, playing "We're an American Band" by Grand Funk Railroad.

They both sang along during the chorus, neither knowing the lyrics to the verses very well.

This wasn't their first trip down the Natchez Trace. They were sent here several times in previous months to find the plants their little group would need to supplement what they were growing on the farm. They had already scoped out most places with available parking, from the Meriwether Lewis stop to Jackson Falls. Their destination for today was the Gordon House. The Gordon House and its surrounding property had just been purchased this year by the National Parks Service to be added as a historical site to visit along the Trace. Robbie and August were anxious to see what the fuss was all about.

They pulled off the road into a makeshift parking lot. Construction of the new historic site had not yet been started. From their vantage point, they could see the ruins of what was once the home of Captain John Gordon and his family, built from 1817 to 1818. Robbie parked the bus, and the two got out, bringing four five-gallon buckets with them as they came. They walked along the edge of the field around the house, looking for mint, lavender, or other herbs useful to their clan. They found a hickory tree sitting next to the river bearing nuts that were not yet ripe for harvesting. They made a mental note to come back in the fall.

They walked along the riverbank, gleaning any plant life they could. Eventually, they found themselves in an open field of about forty acres. The field lacked any useful foliage, except maybe broom sage that grew tall and golden. They walked through the field, crossing the other side where the forest began. As they entered the forest, they saw a shimmering light up ahead. Curious, they moved forward to inspect the light. August said, "Man, Robbie! What is it?"

"Far out!" said Robbie. "I think it's the stairway to heaven, man."

They slowly crept forward until they found themselves on the other side, in another open field. The grass here was lush and green. They wandered about for a bit, eventually splitting away from each other. August found a grove of blackberry vines. They were loaded with blackberries the size of large grapes. He worked steadily at picking the berries, losing track of time and Robbie. Robbie had moved farther into the middle of the open field. August could hear Robbie in the distance, singing to himself in a falsetto voice, "No more Mister Nice Guy. No more Mister Clee he he hean."

Then suddenly, August heard, "Hey, man, what are you doing out..." Then August heard a choking sound and then coughing. Then he heard someone yell in what sounded like a war cry from an old John Wayne western. He looked up from behind the blackberry vines to see his friend as he fell to the ground after being run through by a long spear with feathers hanging from one end. August quickly ducked into concealment, hoping that he had not been spotted by the red savage who rode atop a brown horse painted with white and black stripes. The red man raised his fist in victory as he screamed a warrior's yell. Then he turned his mount back into the field and returned from where he had come.

August was paralyzed by fear. He dared not move from the briars he lay in, even though they were piercing through his clothing and causing him to bleed. He couldn't believe what he had just witnessed. Was it true? Did he see an Indian kill his best friend? Were there Indians roaming through this area in 1973? *Am I dreaming?* he thought. *Maybe I'm on a bad trip. This whole expedition is just an illusion.* August remained in his hiding place until dark. He waited, and he cried.

CHAPTER 1

December 20, 2017: Vroom! The old Long Life Vehicle moved forward to its next box. Daniel looked to his left and fingered the mail while silently reading the names of the occupants of box 1631 Williamson Dr. "*Cooper, Cooper, Cooper... oops, that one doesn't go here.*"

He placed the missorted piece of mail in the four-compartment tray at his side. Once he got back to the post office, it would be sorted through, along with all the other pieces of undeliverable mail. He placed the deliverable mail into the mailbox, then shut the box lid and pulled away to the next box.

Daniel Lane was a good-looking young man of thirty who stood 6'2". He was well-built but not overly athletic. Daniel had never intended to be a mail carrier. It just happened. History was his thing. He had loved history since he was a small boy. He had been homeschooled by his mother, and part of that schooling meant visiting all the historic sites around the Middle Tennessee area—Stones River State Park in Murfreesboro; the Carter House and the Carnton Plantation in Franklin; Nashboro Village in downtown Nashville; Rippa Villa in Columbia; and his favorite, the Natchez Trace Parkway. He was particularly fond of the Parkway because of a book he found at an early age while visiting a souvenir shop at Nashboro Village. It was a history about the Trace and those who lived along it, written by a man with whom he shared a name. "**A History of the People who lived along the Natchez Trail**" by Daniel Lane. Daniel had asked his mother and his father if this writer might be a relative. Neither knew of anyone in the family by that name. It didn't matter. Daniel felt as if he had made a special connection with this writer. The book was his prized possession as a boy. He must have read it a hundred times.

The love of that book and all the many historical sites he had visited as a boy led him to study history when he attended Lipscomb University later in life. It was there he met Emily Crockett, a beautiful young woman from Lawrenceburg, Tennessee, who was studying to be a nurse. After graduation, they married and made their home in Columbia. Emily worked at the local hospital, while Daniel took a job as a history teacher at one of the high schools. It wasn't long before Daniel discovered teaching was not his calling. The kids weren't interested in learning, and Daniel had no patience in dealing with them. He decided he could make more money and pursue his own interests by following in his father's footsteps. So, he became a rural mail carrier. Daniel worked four years at the Columbia Post Office as a part-time carrier before going full-time. Once he reached career status, he and Emily bought a small ten-acre farm in Hampshire, Tennessee, just nine miles from the Columbia Post Office. Daniel and Emily wanted to live a simple life. They were interested in growing their own food while getting back to the basics. Emily was also interested in natural remedies. She studied aromatherapy and herbal remedies. Daniel said on more than one occasion that he wanted to "live a simpler life and live it to the fullest."

The weather in Columbia, Tennessee, was unusually warm for this time of year. They were still experiencing 70-degree days. Daniel was still dressed in his normal summer gear, a T-shirt and shorts. As he continued to deliver his route, he noticed a white sedan in his side-view mirror. He had seen the vehicle earlier in the day and didn't like the vibe he was now feeling as he made his way down Williamson Drive. The car was keeping its distance, but it was definitely following him. *More than likely, he thought it was a supervisor doing a carrier observation. Just make sure you don't do anything against regulations, and everything will be all right.* As he continued his route, he made certain he did everything by the book. When he stopped to dismount for a package delivery, he set his handbrake, cocked his wheels to-ward the curb, turned off the ignition, removed the keys from the steering column, and unbuckled his seat belt. He normally did these things anyway, but he wasn't taking any chances now.

As he turned right onto Eskew Drive, he glanced back and noticed the vehicle following him had not been issued by the postal service after all. There was a dent in the car's passenger door, and the front tag was not that of a Federal Government vehicle. It was a civilian's vehicle. Two individuals were in the car—one white male and one African American male. When he turned right onto Joel Drive, he saw they continued to lag behind. Now, he was suspicious of the sedan. Not because they might be checking his procedures but because it was almost Christmas and people had been known to follow postal vehicles as well as UPS and FedEx vehicles as they delivered packages to the door. Then, they would steal the packages after the delivery person had dropped them off. They had come to be known as "Porch Pirates."

Daniel decided to make a little detour to gather some information on the vehicle. He continued down Joel Drive, discontinuing delivery tem-porarily. He then made a quick left on Avers Avenue and proceeded back to Eskew Drive, going around the block. He pulled up behind the white vehicle and started his dismount procedures when the sedan quickly pulled away, but not before Daniel could get a look at the license plate. Tennessee tag R12 56P. He jotted down the tag number on a sticky note and then called his supervisor to inform her of the situation. "Columbia Post Office, Barbara speaking."

"Barbara," Daniel said. "I've got—"

Suddenly, the white sedan sped toward Daniel from behind. He saw them coming through the side mirror on the left side. The car pulled up on the left side of the LLV and quickly stopped. There in the passenger seat, a young white man with a shaved head and scraggly beard raised a handgun and fired three times into the left window of the LLV. Glass from the window that had only been rolled down halfway exploded in on Daniel while he was in mid-sentence. He instinctively ducked sideways to his right, and only his seat belt kept him from rolling out of the postal truck. Daniel yelled into the phone, "I'm hit, I'm hit!"

Barbara Jones, with wide eyes and a shaky voice, yelled back. "Daniel! Where are you?"

The sedan then sped away, squealing tires as it did. "I'm on Joel Drive! Send help!"

With a quiver in her voice, Barbara softly spoke to him and said, "Hang on. Help's on the way." Without hanging up the receiver, Barbara punched the button for line 2 on the telephone and deliberately dialed 911.

Daniel placed the gear shift of the LLV in Park, set the handbrake, and turned off the ignition. His heart was racing, and his adrenaline was high. He then slowly unbuckled his lap belt, which had kept him from falling out of the opened door of the truck as he had dodged the bullets. As he tried to step out of the truck, he felt himself wobbling as he climbed down onto the asphalt. He sat down on the step of the LLV, dropped his head between his knees, and waited. He noticed some blood dripping from his left arm onto the ground but held his position. He felt that if he moved, he might throw up.

It seemed like hours had passed, although it had only taken ten minutes for two police cruisers to show up. After another five minutes, the ambulance and three other police personnel drove up. The first officer to approach Daniel was a short, heavyset man with a crew cut. Daniel looked up dizzily at the officer when he spoke and noticed a large wart on the side of his head. It made him think of his football coach back in the Pop Warner League he had played in as a boy. Coach White had worn the same style crew cut and had the same type of wart on the side of his head. Daniel had always wondered how the coach managed to keep his hair cut so short without cutting that wart off with the hair clippers. "You all right, buddy?" the officer asked.

"Yeah, I think so," Daniel replied. "But I'm feeling a little queasy."

The officer then asked, "Can you tell me what happened?"

Daniel explained what had happened to the officer and then handed him the sticky note he still held in his hand. The officer took the sticky note with the car tag number jotted on it. Then, he returned to his cruiser to check the tag number.

Two EMTs—one male and one female—came to Daniel to examine him for injuries. The woman attached a blood pressure cup to his left arm and checked his blood pressure. Daniel winced as the Velcro band tightened around his arm. "One-fifty over ninety-eight," she said. "It's a little high, but that's to be expected. How do you feel?" she asked.

"A little dizzy, but not as bad as I was earlier," he answered.

The male EMT was constantly tugging at Daniel, checking him for injuries. "I don't see any bullet holes," he said. "Just a lot of cuts from that shattered window, I think.

Just then, Daniel noticed a Transit van drive up. It was one of the newer cargo vans that many car manufacturers were selling now. This one had the postal service logo on it. Out stepped Barbara Jones, Daniel's supervisor, with a fearful look on her face. Stephanie Sutton, one of the postal maintenance crew, was with her. As Barbara made her way over to where Daniel was seated, Stephanie began to pull mail trays, parcels, and all other equipment out of the LLV and load them into the cargo van. Daniel asked, "Do you have another LLV for me? I think I'm okay to finish the route."

"Oh, no," Barbara said, "you're going to the hospital to get checked out. I'll have some of the subs split up the rest of your route when they come back from their routes."

"Well, do I have to go to the hospital?" Daniel asked. "I feel fine!"

"Yep!" she replied. "Hospital, accident report, the whole shebang! I'm also putting you on administrative leave until Monday unless the doctor says different."

Daniel breathed a deep sigh and let it go. Just then, Stephanie walked up to Daniel, gave him his cell phone, and said, "Here. Are you okay, Daniel?"

"Yeah, I'm fine." He huffed. "Thanks, Steph!"

A tow truck pulled into the scene and backed up to the LLV. The vehicle was towed back to the post office parking lot, where it would be left until someone from vehicle maintenance from Nashville could come and replace the broken window on the left side. Daniel was loaded into the ambulance and sent on his way to Columbia General Hospital, the only hospital in town.

Barbara and Stephanie got back into the van and drove back to the post office to distribute the remaining mail and parcels to the substitute carriers as they returned from their routes. Then Barbara got back in the van and drove to the emergency room so she could get all the details for her report.

As the ambulance began pulling away, Daniel realized he hadn't contacted his wife, Emily. She'd kill him if he didn't give her the heads up on something like this. He pulled out his cell phone and found her number, then hit the dial button. She would find out soon enough since she was a nurse in the hospital's emergency department. But he still thought he'd better let her know he was all right. Her phone went straight to voicemail. Rather than leaving a message, Daniel chose to hang up and send her a text.

"Had a little accident. On my way to ER. I'm OK."

Emily read the text and suddenly got a sinking feeling in her stomach. She informed her supervisor what was about to happen and then stood by the entrance of the ER. Ten minutes later, the ambulance arrived. The EMTs wheeled Daniel out of the ambulance and rolled him through the automatic doors of the ER. Emily greeted them all and escorted them back to room 4. They were about to move him from the gurney onto the bed when Daniel stopped them. "I'm not that hurt." he snapped. "I can get over there by myself."

They all froze as if they had each been shot. Daniel hopped off the gurney and moved over to the bed. Once he was settled on the examining table, the EMTs left the room. Emily began cleaning Daniel's wounds and then looked him straight in the eyes, "What happened?" she asked.

Daniel gave her the whole story, wincing now and then when Emily removed a piece of glass from his left arm or the left side of his face.

A young doctor named Martin Williams came in and asked Daniel a few questions. He poked Daniel's belly, listened to his heart and lungs, and proclaimed Daniel to be OK. "You're dealing with a little shock," he said. "But you'll be fine. We'll get you out of here real soon." Then he walked out of the room.

Just then, Barbara walked into the room. "You feel like helping me fill out this report?" she asked.

"Yeah, let's get this over with," Daniel replied.

Emily gathered up her things and began to leave the room. "I'll get the discharge paperwork started," she announced. "Then I'll come back and take you home."

"No need," Daniel said. "I can catch a ride back to the office with Barbara and get my truck. You go ahead and finish your shift. I'll be fine."

"My shift *is* finished," she replied.

Barbara stood there with her mouth open, watching their conversation go back and forth as if she were at a tennis match.

"I'm going to make sure you get home OK," Emily said. "But I *need* my truck," Daniel returned.

"I'll *take* you to the office, so you can get your truck. Then I'll follow you home," she replied.

"All right. Sounds good to me," Daniel conceded.

The plan was set. Barbara got her paperwork filled out. Daniel made it home in one piece with his truck. Emily pulled into the driveway close behind Daniel. It was four o'clock. The sun was starting to fade behind the treetops. When Emily exited her car, Daniel hugged her and said, "Thanks!"

"No problem," she replied. "I'm gonna get some supper started."

"All right," said Daniel. "I'll take care of the animals."

Daniel grabbed a stainless steel bucket from the garage, moved to the house's north side, walked twenty yards, and came to a big red pipe gate. He opened the gate and began walking through the pasture. As he continued up the hill, three white goats, a nanny, and two kids raised their heads from nibbling on some dried leaves on the ground. They all greeted Daniel with a *maah*, then stampeded toward him. They followed him up to the barn and waited impatiently for him to get started. He hung the bucket on a nail on a barn post, then moved over to the left side, where the chickens were already beginning to roost for the night.

The barn wasn't big. It was divided into five stalls. One of them was a double-sized stall. That's where the chickens were kept. This stall had rock walls. An outside door on the south wall allowed Daniel to enter the coop, and another on the west wall led into a run covered completely in chicken wire. The run allowed the chickens to roam around outside without fear of predators. The two middle stalls of the barn were divided by a wall of goat wire. This kept the goats from jumping through and getting into the feed Daniel had stored in the back stall. The last two stalls were one big stall with a gate in the middle, allowing it to be used for a large animal if needed or for smaller animals if the gate was closed.

Daniel checked for eggs in the nesting boxes. There were only two eggs—typical for this time of year. He gathered them up and put them in the pocket of the windbreaker he was wearing. Hopefully, he wouldn't forget they were there when he returned to the house. He made sure there was plenty of food and water in the coop, then stepped out of the coop and secured the door. He then moved to the last stalls and walked through to the back gate of the stall. This led him to the second pasture, where the horses were kept. Two barrel-chested bays trotted up to Daniel as he distributed hay into the hayrack that hung on the east wall of the barn. As they began to pull at the hay, Daniel checked the mare. She was pregnant and due to foal in early April. Satisfied with her, Daniel walked from the barn to a third pasture divided into two large pens. These pens held his hogs. They were full-bred Berkshires—black hogs with white markings, sometimes on their legs and feet. Each pen held three hogs. One boar and two sows. He wanted to keep them separate so no inbreeding would occur. Eventually, new boars would replace these to keep the bloodlines clean. There was no need to feed these animals. They were grazers, eating grass, roots, acorns, and whatever else they might find while foraging through their pens. A small creek ran through the middle of the pasture, so they had plenty of fresh water.

After checking on the hogs, Daniel returned to the barn and secured the two kid goats in one of the middle stalls, separating them from the nanny, who was locked up in the last stall. She was close enough to them so they would not be stressed, but they couldn't get to her at night. This allowed Emily to come in the next morning and milk the nanny. Once she was milked, the kids were released back into the pasture with her to nurse during the day. The milk Emily took from the nanny was enough to share with friends and all their needs.

Daniel strolled back to the house, taking his time, when his cell phone rang. He pulled it out of his back pants pocket and checked it. The display read "Jimbo."

James Robert Gleason was Daniel's best friend. They grew up together for a while in Columbia, then reconnected after college. Jimbo had a small farm just up the road on Cathey's Creek Road. His place was just big enough for him: his dog, Jake; his cat, Jinx, and his sorrel gelding, Rusty.

"What's up, Jimbo?" Daniel said on the phone.

"Hey, buddy," Jimbo sang back to him. "We still own fer t'morra?"

"You bet," Daniel replied. "How does nine o'clock sound?"

"Sounds great!" Jimbo replied. "See ya then."

Daniel smiled as he hung up and continued to walk to the house. He and Jimbo had been planning a trail ride for a couple of weeks. Tomorrow was the day. They would take their horses up to the Natchez Trace and do some exploring. The weather was going to be perfect for it.

Daniel could smell the aroma of dinner in the air as he entered the house. Emily had prepared a quick meal of spaghetti and meat sauce. "Mm... smells good," Daniel said. "Hey, Em. Did you remember about tomorrow?" he asked.

"The trail ride, you mean?" she responded. "How could I forget? You and Jimmy have been going on about it for two weeks." Emily refused to call a grown man Jimbo. Emily was a strong-willed woman. She was strong in her beliefs, and she had little patience for incompetent people. She was fairly tall by most people's standards. She was 5'10", with mousy brown shoulder-length hair and a beautiful face that would challenge most models. Many of the men who visited the hospital's emergency department also noticed her beauty. She had very little patience for those who thought it necessary to make advances toward her. She often took it out on them whenever there was a need to stick a needle in their rump or their arm. She could be gentle when the need arose. But she saw no need to be gentle with those she deemed undeserving.

"Do you care if I still go?" Daniel asked. "I mean, after what happened today?"

Emily walked over to him, wrapped her arms around his waist, and pulled him toward her. "I think it'll be good for you," she said. "Just make sure you get home before dark, okay?"

Daniel replied, "Don't worry. I will."

~~~~~~~~~~~~~~~~~~~

The 1996 white Ford Taurus pulled into the driveway of a duplex on Stanfill Drive. The driver, Maurice Williams, was a large African American man—6'2" tall and 275 pounds. Maurice, also known as Mo, got out of the car and stretched as if he had been driving for hours. He looked around the neighborhood, checking to see if anyone had followed them. He cocked his head, listening for any approaching vehicles. "Aeeght, let's go," he said to the passenger.

The passenger, Jimmy Wakefield, was of much smaller stature. He was only 5'7" and weighed a wiry 135 pounds. As Jimmy got out of the car, he slid his 9 mm Beretta into the back waistband of his baggy jeans. Each man opened the back door on either side of the car to remove the packages they had picked up throughout the morning and early afternoon. The smaller boxes were sacked away in large plastic shopping bags. Two of the packages were too large to hide in the bags. They would have to carry them into the house in plain sight. When they got into the house, they emptied the bags on a small folding table used as a dining table for this sparsely furnished duplex unit. They counted twelve packages—two FedEx packages, one large UPS package, and nine that the United States Postal Service had delivered.

Jimmy said, "Let's see what we got, man!"

Each man pulled a switchblade knife from his back pocket and opened the package nearest him. Mo opened a small FedEx box. Inside, he found a Motorola G cell phone. "Cool, baby!" he said. "We scored on that hit. Cell phone, baby!"

"Ah, man!" Jimmy replied. "I hope they all that good." Jimmy opened his first package. Inside was a toy bulldozer. Jimmy cursed, "Man, that's wack. People cain't buy no crap better than this?"

Mo chuckled and said, "Hey, save it, man. My little boy will play with it."

Mo opened the next package. "Oh, yeah, baby!" he said. "Sony Bluetooth headphones."

Jimmy's eyes lit up. "Ah, man. Them is sweet, baby!"

The two continued unboxing their take until it was all unpacked. In all, their cache was the cell phone, Bluetooth headphones, the toy bulldozer, a Fitbit, a Harry Potter T-shirt, a pair of Nike running shoes, a Paw Patrol action figure set, a Clinique seven-piece gift set, a BMX 14″ bike with training wheels, a Proctor Silex Pro-Style electric deep fryer, a Star Wars coffee mug collector set, and a 9.7″ iPad case with camo print. Mo would keep and give the toys and the bike to his son, while the more sellable items they would fence at a local pawn shop or sell on eBay.

Jimmy said, "Hey, man let's go out and get some more while it's still daylight."

"Naw, man, I cain't," responded Mo. "I gots ta pick up my son from school. Cum own, I'll drop you off on duh way."

At the end of the street was an unmarked police car. Inside sat Sergeant Jason Rawley. "All units, the subjects are coming out of the house. Stand by!"

A patrol unit was around the corner and behind Sergeant Rawley, ready and waiting. On the opposite end of Stanfill Drive were two more cruisers parked on Zion Road and out of sight. In case the two men tried to run on foot, two more units were parked on Napier Drive, one block over from Stanfill. Rawley announced over the radio, "Subjects are getting into the white Taurus. They're backing out, and they'll be heading east on Stanfill."

Mo and Jimmy proceeded down Stanfill Drive with their radio thumping out an indiscernible tune. Neither man was aware of the trap that had been laid for them.

"Go, go, go!" the call came over the police radio. Sergeant Rawley's car pulled up behind the Taurus, and the other patrol car pulled up next to him so that both street lanes were blocked. Ahead of the Taurus, two other patrol cars came in from Zion Road, side by side, heading straight for the men. The two men each cursed when they realized what was happening. Mo slammed on the brakes, and the Taurus came to a halt twenty feet from the approaching cars. He jammed the gear shift lever into reverse, then looked back and saw two other cars were parked eight feet behind him. Mo looked at Jimmy and said, "Dey got us, man!"

"They ain't got me!" Jimmy exclaimed.

Mo was too large to get out of the car quickly, but Jimmy leaped from the car and ran as fast as his wiry legs would carry him. Rawley reached up to the radio mic attached to the epaulet on his uniform and called out, "We've got a rabbit, headed toward Napier."

An answer came back over the radio, "Ten-four."

Mo slowly extracted himself from the Taurus with his hands raised high. Without instructions from the officers, he lay facedown and spread-eagle on the asphalt road. He knew the routine. The officers were yelling at him, but he knew what to do. He had been here before. Possession of marijuana and disorderly conduct had landed him in county lockup before. Two of the officers approached Mo and searched him while the sergeant held him at gunpoint. They cuffed him using zip tie cuffs, then loaded him into the back of one of the cruisers.

Jimmy ran between two houses and jumped a chain-link fence in the backyard of one of the houses. Two black and tan dachshunds chased Jimmy through the yard, nipping at his feet and barking all the while. Jimmy eyed his exit—a privacy fence at the back of the property. He measured it in his mind. I got this! he thought. He jumped and reached for the top of the six-foot fence and swung his feet up over the top in one motion. When he landed on the other side, he was greeted by a large German shepherd K-9 officer who pulled against the leash of his partner while angrily barking at Jimmy.

"Facedown, on the ground!" yelled one of the officers. Jimmy complied and lay facedown in a moist clump of grass.

While cuffing and frisking him, one of the officers found the 9 mm handgun in the waistband of Jimmy's jeans. "Well, looky here," the officer said. "Now, I don't suppose you have a carry permit for this, do you?"

Being careful not to damage any fingerprints on the weapon, he sniffed the gun and said, "It's been fired recently." He removed the magazine from the handle and examined its contents. "Four rounds missing."

The two officers picked Jimmy up and escorted him to one of the cruisers. One of them said, "Well, Jimmy, looks like there's good news and bad news. The bad news is you're under arrest. The good news is you'll have free room and board for quite a while." The other officer read Jimmy his Miranda rights as they led him away.

CHAPTER 2

December 21, 2017: Daniel awoke to the sound of Emily milling around in the bathroom, getting ready for work. It was 6:00 a.m., and she had to be at work by 7:00. Daniel poked his head through the bathroom door and announced, "I'll take care of the milking for you today."

She continued to apply her makeup while looking in the mirror but replied, "Thanks! That will be a big help."

He knew she would be leaving before he could return from the barn, so he grabbed and hugged her, then kissed her goodbye. "See ya tonight," he said. He released her, headed back into the bedroom, put on his clothes, and headed toward the barn.

Daniel walked up the rise to the barn and was immediately greeted by the goats with their "*Maaa.*" He ignored them for now, then walked to the next pasture to check on the horses and hogs. Everyone was okay. He returned to the barn, opened the door to the coop, walked inside, gathered six eggs from the nesting boxes, and then placed the eggs in the pockets of his jacket. He then walked over to the stall where the nanny goat was caged. He went inside and walked over to the milking stanchion. He poured a couple of small scoops of sweet feed into the feeder situated on the front of the stanchion. The nanny hopped onto the stanchion and slipped her head through the head chute so she could reach the feed. As she greedily began munching on the feed, Daniel locked her head in place so she couldn't move from the stanchion. He grabbed the stainless steel bucket and a container of baby wipes from the shelf above his head and sat on a stool placed next to the stanchion. Daniel cleaned the nanny's two teats with one of the baby wipes, then placed the bucket beneath her belly and began stroking the teats and squeezing out the milk into the bucket. He took just enough without stripping her completely of milk. He would save some for the kids. When he was finished, he released the nanny into the front pasture and opened the stall door where the kids were kept overnight to allow them to rejoin their mother. They went straight for their mother and began nursing right away. Daniel took one more look around the barn and pastures. Satisfied that all was good for the day, he trudged back down the slope toward the house.

Once in the house, he washed the eggs he had collected and filtered the milk, pouring it into a half-gallon glass jar. He then twisted the lid onto the jar and put it in the refrigerator. He stuck a bagel into the toaster and made a cup of coffee in the Keurig, swallowed it all down quickly, and then headed into the bedroom to get ready for the day.

Daniel realized the TV was on in the den as he stepped out of the shower and began to dry off. Sports Center. That meant Jimbo had let himself in. James Robert Gleason had been Daniel's closest friend from the age of twelve when Daniel moved into the area. He didn't like the name James or Robert, and especially not Jim Bob, which his dad had tried to name him from a character from an old TV show he used to watch as a boy. So he made sure everyone knew his name was Jimbo—everyone except Emily. She was the only one he allowed to call him anything else. She preferred Jimmy. He was thirty-three, not handsome, tall and lean, and usually needed a haircut and a shave. He wasn't married, at least, not now. He once was married to an eighteen-year-old girl five years younger than him. It didn't last a year. She quickly discovered she wasn't cut out for living in the country. It was too dirty. There was too much work to be done on the farm. Jimbo wasn't ambitious enough. He was educated, so why couldn't he go out and get a real job so they would have more money? After eight months of nagging and complaining, Jimbo had had enough. He packed her things into large black garbage bags, shoved them into the back seat of her Ford Escort, and showed her the door. He vowed he would never make that mistake again. He would live out the rest of his life a confirmed bachelor. He would live alone, except for his dog, Jake, and his ginger tom cat, Jinx.

"Be right out!" Daniel shouted toward the den. As he turned toward the mirror to begin shaving, Jake came into the room and greeted Daniel by poking him in the backside with his nose. With a grunt, Daniel responded, "Nice to smell you too, Jake." Jake stared up at Daniel while wagging his tail furiously in response. Daniel finished shaving, then went into the bedroom and got dressed. He then walked into the den and found Jimbo munching on something. "Ya hungry?" Daniel asked.

"Naw, man. I found a bag of chocolate donuts in the pantry. Hope you don't mind," Jimbo replied.

Daniel spoke again, "Naw, that's okay. Ya want some milk to wash it down?"

Jimbo responded, "Naw, man. I don't drink that healthy stuff. I got me a coke."

Daniel said, "Well, let's go then. We're burning daylight."

They headed outside to where Jimbo's truck and horse trailer were waiting. Daniel tossed his saddlebags into the truck cab. They contained their lunch and other items he thought might be needed on their trail ride. Emily insisted on a first aid kit. There was also bottled water, a thermos of coffee, a flashlight, a hunting knife, and a compass. Daniel then walked back up to the barn and retrieved the big bay stud that he had named Hoss. He led Hoss to the shed behind the house. Inside the shed was a room that served as a tack room. Daniel changed out the halter Hoss was wearing with a bridle, then threw a blanket and saddle on the horse's back and cinched it, but not tightly. They loaded Hoss up in the trailer next to Jimbo's horse,

Rusty, then lowered the truck's tailgate so Jake could get in. They were now ready for their winter solstice trail ride along the Natchez Trace.

The truck and trailer pulled out onto the road and turned right. They drove for two miles until the road came to a dead end. They then turned right again onto Highway 412 and headed west toward the Trace. After fifteen minutes of driving, they came to a community called Gordonsburg. It really wasn't even a community. It was a spot on the road where a Church of Christ stood on the right and a small campground just a little farther down on the right. They immediately slowed the truck. Across the road from the campground was the entrance ramp to the Natchez Trace Parkway. They followed the ramp, which looped to the right, then stopped. If they turned left, they would head south toward Alabama and then cross into Mississippi. About 340 miles later, they'd be in Natchez. Instead, they turned north toward Nashville. They would drive about 18 miles to an area called Shady Grove.

Along the way, they passed all the popular stops tourists explore while going down the Trace. They passed by Fall Hollow, which featured a walking trail that wound through groves of small cedar, hackberry, and hickory trees. The trees grew up through outcroppings of Tennessee limestone that seemed to be piled up just so. The trail could be difficult to maneuver through at times. The trail moved downhill, winding around. At times, it seemed it wasn't really a trail at all. But now and again, there would be a boardwalk showing the way. Sometimes, the boardwalk would provide a small seating area where people could rest along the way. Eventually, the trail ended at the bottom of a thirty-foot bluff, where water flowed over the top and landed into a small pool overflowing into a tiny little creek. It was pretty but not all that impressive once you had seen it a few times.

They passed other spots along the way that Daniel had visited in the past at one point in time or another—the Devil's Backbone, Old Trace, Baker Bluff Overlook. But one of his favorites was a place called Sheboss Place. There wasn't anything to see there. The stop called Sheboss Place wasn't necessarily the actual location of Sheboss Place. In the early 1800s, the United States government made a deal with the chief of the Chickasaw Indians that would allow for a road to be built from Nashville to Natchez. Along this road, stands were built at intervals one day apart. The stands could only be owned or run by people belonging to the Chickasaw nation or their relatives. Sheboss Place was one of those stands. A stand, also known as an inn, allowed travelers to find places of refuge during travel along what was then known as the Natchez Road. This stand got its name because the owner, a Chickasaw man, was married to a white woman who had been widowed. No one seemed to know who she was or where the exact location of the stand was. Whenever someone traveling down the road stopped to check on accommodations for the night and approached the man, he pointed to the woman and exclaimed, "She boss!"

Jackson Falls was the next stop along the way. Jackson Falls is the real thing. It's quite a hike to the falls, circling them from the top and going down to the bottom by way of a concrete sidewalk at times and a dirt trail the rest of the time. The falls drop three hundred feet below the parking lot's surface, which serves as the entrance to the spectacle. It is one of the more popular places to visit along the Trace.

When the two men passed the entrance to the Gordon House, they knew they were almost at their destination. The Gordon House was built in 1817–1818 as a home site for ferry operator John Gordon, who had made a deal with Chickasaw chief Willam Colbert. Gordon had begun operating the ferry that crossed the Duck River in 1802, along with a trading post. He later moved his family down from Nashville to construct their new home.

The home was a federal-style building with a red brick exterior, which was rare along the frontier. Shortly after starting construction on the home, Gordon was called away to fight with General Andrew Jackson. His wife, Dolly, would oversee the finishing of the project as well as their ferry, trading post, and farming businesses. John Gordon died shortly after the home was completed.

The truck and trailer exited the Trace to the left and entered a parking lot about half an acre in size. No other vehicles were there. They would have the place to themselves. They drove to the back of the lot and parked. Daniel and Jimbo stepped out of the truck and stretched to remove the kinks from their joints. They then proceeded to relieve themselves on either side of the truck. It would be a long day on horseback and neither wanted to make it more uncomfortable by riding with a full bladder.

Jake jumped from the back of the truck and quickly and excitedly began traveling back and forth along the edge of the pavement with his nose to the ground, searching furiously for something unseen. He settled on a tree just inside the clearing where the parking lot lay. He circled the tree, sniffing all the while, then stopped. With his head held high, he raised his back leg and marked his spot. "Jake!" Jimbo called. Jake loped back toward the truck, tail wagging and tongue hanging out the side of his mouth. He looked like he was very pleased with himself. Daniel and Jimbo unloaded the two horses from the trailer, then checked the saddles and cinched them tight. Each man retrieved their saddlebags from the truck and tied them to the back of the saddles. They secured the truck and trailer, then mounted the horses and moved toward a trail south of their position.

Daniel pulled out his cell phone from his back pocket and checked the time. "Ten o'clock," he said. "We've got about five hours before we need to be back here and head home. I promised Em I'd be home before dark."

"Well, okay then, lets git," Jimbo replied.

The two men began riding through the trees, down a path that the National Park Service had cut out. Dried leaves crumbled under their horses' hooves and under Jake's feet as he scouted the trail, sometimes leading and sometimes trailing behind. A mild breeze feathered their faces as they moved methodically through the leafless stands of oak, hickory, and hackberry. The trail moved south toward the Duck River, and after thirty minutes of riding, they could hear its waters flowing, moving westerly to easterly. At this point, the trail wouldn't take them all the way to the riverbank. They would be on a high bluff above the river. Too dangerous to get very close. They would continue to ride east until they could find a safer place to spy the river. They eventually came to a place on the trail under the Parkway. It was a bridge that towered over the Duck from bluff to bluff. Soon, their ride began to move down a hill. The river was closer now. They could smell the odor of mussels that would be resting on the banks of the river. Over to their left, a clearing was exposed. In the clearing was the old Gordon House. Not far away, they could see the parking lot of the exhibit, where a couple had left their car to use the restrooms. Farther up the trail was their destination. A field opened up behind the house. At some point, what had been a pasture was now an open field of tall broom straw sage.

At the far end of the field, the two would pick up the trail and then move even farther east. Suddenly, Jake let out a slight woof. The horses snorted and tensed. Off to their left stood a deer at the edge of the trees. It was at least forty yards away. Without notice, Jake jumped into action, leaping toward his prey at full speed, rumbling and growling as he darted through the tall, dry grass. "No!" yelled Jimbo. "Jake, come back here you, idget!" Jimbo reined his horse to the left and kicked him in the side to move him forward. The horse bounded into a gallop, chasing Jake as the dog ducked into a grove of tall cedars.

Daniel muttered to himself, "That's just great! We'll never find that stupid dog in them trees." He turned his horse and followed but at a much slower pace. Daniel saw Jake jump into the grove of cedars, and then, closely behind, was Jimbo on his horse. A moment later, they all disappeared from Daniel's sight.

Daniel reached the grove and noticed a strange shimmering light inside the forest. As he moved in closer, he saw Jimbo and his horse jumping into the light, then vanishing. What is that? he thought. The strange light reminded Daniel of heat waves moving along the ground in the desert or on hot pavement in the summer. He couldn't see past the frame of light. He couldn't see into it, either. He knew that more trees stood on the other side of the light, but they weren't visible. "Jimbo!" he yelled. No answer. "Jimbo!" he called again. Still no answer. Daniel slowly moved Hoss forward toward the light frame. He thought he could hear something through the light. It sounded like yelling. *Jimbo*! he thought. He kicked Hoss in the sides, and they jumped through the light. A cold sensation moved through Daniel's body as they landed on the other side.

What is this? he thought. The land seemed different. The temperature had dropped, at least by twenty degrees. He expected to land in the grove of trees, but it was an open field—at least forty acres. Large rocks were scattered around the field, but very few trees. However, the field was surrounded by forest. Up ahead, Daniel spotted Jimbo. He heard him yelling and saw him waving his arms around like he was trying to scare something off. Daniel looked around the area and saw why Jimbo was yelling. Three men on horseback were riding toward Jimbo. Daniel spoke aloud. "What the—Are those Indians?" Daniel's eyes widened in terror as he saw one of the men raise a long pole in the air as he raced toward Jimbo. Only, it wasn't a pole. It was a lance. Daniel gasped as he watched the lance fly straight into Jimbo's chest as Jimbo screamed. Jimbo fell from Rusty's back as the three men rode toward him, captured the horse, and then rode in the opposite direction.

Daniel pulled his cell phone from his pocket and checked for a signal. No bars. They evidently were too far from any towers. So he waited. He didn't know if the men had heard him yell for Jimbo or not. He didn't dare to approach Jimbo until he was sure they were gone. After what seemed like fifteen minutes, he noticed some movement in the trees behind Jimbo's body. Daniel tensed as he felt his adrenaline flowing through his body. Had the men come back? He shrunk to the ground, holding onto the reins of his horse. Hoss's ears raised slightly as he tugged against Daniel's grip on the reins. The horse snorted. Daniel quickly raised his body and placed his free hand over the horse's muzzle to quiet him. What was Hoss seeing? The light was fading now. It must be about 4:30, he thought. But he could just barely make out a shadow of movement behind Jimbo. *Jake*! he thought.

Daniel led his horse around the edge of the field next to the trees, moving clockwise toward Jimbo. He moved slowly but deliberately, stopping whenever he heard a twig snap or a rock fall. As he approached the body, he saw that the shadow was indeed Jake. The dog lay over the body of his master, whimpering. "Jake," Daniel whispered loudly. Jake cocked his eyes at Daniel. But he didn't move from his position. When he recognized Daniel, he wagged his tail twice. Then, returned to his whimpers. Daniel tied Hoss to the limb of a small dogwood tree at the edge of the field, only twelve feet away from where his friend lay. When he reached Jimbo, Daniel saw he wasn't dead. But he had lost a lot of blood from his chest where the lance had pierced him, and blood flowed from his mouth and nose.

He was on his right side. The lance was sticking out of his chest and back. He glanced up and saw Daniel coming toward him. "Danny!"

He coughed. More blood sprayed from his mouth. Tears welled up in Daniel's eyes as he knelt next to Jimbo. "Danny! An injun kilt me, Danny! He stolt my horse."

"It'll be okay, Jimbo," Daniel whispered. "I'm gonna get you home."

Then, Jimbo gasped and took his last breath.

CHAPTER 3

Emily pulled up to the mailbox directly across from their house and emptied its contents, tossing them into the passenger seat. She then drove up the chert driveway that led to the garage of their house. Daniel's truck was in the garage, but no lights were on in the house. "Oh, Daniel." She moaned. "Should have known you wouldn't be back before dark." She pulled her cell phone out of her purse and dialed his number. The call went straight to voicemail. She gathered her things out of the car and went into the house. She quickly went into the bedroom and changed into a pair of jeans and an old sweatshirt. Then she thought, Maybe he's up at the barn and hasn't returned to the house yet. She grabbed a flashlight from the garage and trudged up to the barn. She pointed the flashlight toward the barn once she walked through the first gate. There, she saw three sets of orange eyes looking at her. Then she heard them. "*Maaah*!" The nanny and her kids ran toward her with delight, expecting some sort of treat. "Well, I see no one has taken care of you guys yet," Emily said. "Come on, let's get you put up for the night."

When they reached the barn, Emily separated the kids from their mother and latched the gates shut. She glanced into the chicken coop but didn't bother gathering the eggs. She decided they could wait until morning. She shut the door to the coop and then walked to the other side of the barn where the horses were kept. "Daniel!" she sang out.

No one answered, but the mare walked toward Emily, rumbling as she walked. "Where's your buddy?" she said.

The mare bowed her head and snorted in reply. Emily moved the flashlight, spanning the width of the field, searching for Hoss. He was nowhere to be seen. Well, I guess that's it, she thought. They haven't gotten back yet. She grabbed a block of hay from the barn and threw it into the hayrack for the mare, then walked back to the house.

When she got back to the house, she decided not to deal with supper for a man who might not be back in time to eat it. So she grabbed a Hot Pocket from the freezer and nuked it in the microwave. She fixed herself a cup of coffee in the Keurig, then had her meal on the couch. It was a cold night, but she didn't build a fire in the fireplace. Daniel usually did that. Instead, she grabbed one of her grandmother's old quilts and wrapped up in it while she watched Netflix. As episode after episode of Pretty Little Liars played on the TV, she grew more and more worried about Daniel. She knew it wouldn't do any good to call the police because he hadn't been missing for twenty-four hours yet. She decided, instead, to call the hospital. She called the emergency department and asked to speak to the supervising nurse.

"Abby Moore, speaking."

Emily replied, "Abby, this is Emily Lane. I'm a nurse on the day shift."

"Yes, Emily! I remember you. How are you?" she asked.

"I'm a little worried," Emily replied. "My husband was supposed to have returned from a trail ride this evening before dark. It's now, 9:30, and I haven't heard from him. I was wondering if you've had anyone brought in tonight?"

Abby began, "Let me see, what is his name?"

Emily replied, "Daniel. Daniel Lane." Emily could hear the keys of a keyboard being punched as Abby did her search.

"No, Emily," she said. "No one by that name and we haven't had any John Doe's tonight either. Sorry!"

Emily said, "Thanks, Abby! Maybe he'll show up soon."

Emily hit the red button on her phone to hang up, then pushed the play button on her TV remote to watch the next Pretty Little Liars episode.

Only, she didn't watch it. Her eyes were on the screen, but her mind was elsewhere, wondering. Where could he be? Her eyes began watering as she closed them. She cried herself to sleep.

When Emily awoke, she looked at her phone to check the time. It was 6:15 a.m. She quickly jumped up from the couch, looking around. She ran to the bedroom. He wasn't in there. "Daniel?" she called. No answer. She tried his cell phone. It went straight to voicemail again. She called Jimbo's number. Same thing. Her frustration was at its peak. But she realized she could finally call the police. It had been more than twenty-four hours since she had seen him last. So, she decided to call the sheriff's department since they lived in the county.

"Sheriff's department. How may I direct your call?" said a female voice on the line.

"I need to file a missing person's report, please," Emily stated.

Without another word, the call was placed on hold. A few seconds later, Emily heard, "Sergeant White. How may I help you?"

Emily began, "My name is Emily Lane. I need to file a missing person's report, please."

"Is the missing person an adult or child?" the sergeant asked.

"Adult" Emily responded. "He's my husband."

Then the sergeant asked, "When was the last time you saw him?"

Emily replied, "Yesterday at 6 a.m. I've tried several times to call his cell phone, and it went straight to voicemail. I've tried calling his best friend who he was going on a trail ride with yesterday, and his phone did the same thing."

"Okay, well I'll send a deputy out to your house so he can fill out the paperwork, and we'll see if we can't locate him for you. Just let me get your address and phone number, and they'll be out quick as they can."

Emily hung up the phone and decided to check on the animals before the deputy arrived. So she put on a light jacket and walked up to the barn to see how everyone was doing. She threw some hay in the rack for the mare, gathered eggs from the chicken coop, and then milked the goat. She then let the kids out of their stall to be with the nanny and have breakfast. She didn't bother checking on the pigs. They were all pretty self-sufficient. Satisfied all the animals would be okay for the day, she walked back to the house to see if the deputy had arrived yet. Just as she reached the backdoor of the house, a white car with gold and green decals pulled up the driveway and parked. Emily walked straight through the house, from the backdoor to the front, to meet the deputy as he reached the front door.

"Mrs. Lane?" the deputy asked.

"Emily," she offered. "Won't you come in?"

As the deputy entered the house, he announced, "I'm Randy Snell. I understand your husband is missing?"

"Yes, sir," she replied.

"Well then, ma'am, let's see if we can get through this paperwork and find him for you, okay?"

They both sat at the dining room table, and the deputy filled out her personal information at the top of the form when Emily's phone rang.

"Sorry," she said as she glanced at it and saw who it was. The hospital was calling.

"Emily?" a voice came over the phone. "This is Gail."

Gail Matthews was the day shift supervisor in the emergency department where Emily worked. Emily jumped up from her seat at the table and made a number one sign with her index finger to the deputy, who nodded in understanding. She moved into her bedroom for a little more privacy.

"Gail, I'm so sorry. I forgot to call in this morning. My husband is missing. There is a deputy here now, taking a report so they can start searching for him."

"So you won't be coming in today?" Gail questioned.

"No, I'll be taking a personal day," Emily replied.

"Okay, well, I hope you find him," Gail said without concern. I guess we'll see you on Monday, then?"

"I certainly hope so," Emily said. "I'll be sure to let you know if anything changes."

Emily returned to the table and sat down. "I'm so sorry," she apologized to the deputy. "I forgot to call the hospital and let them know I wasn't coming in today."

Deputy Snell continued with his questions, such as, "What kind of vehicle were they driving?"

"A white pick-up truck pulling a horse trailer."

"Do you have any idea where they were going?"

"We usually park at the Shady Grove exit off the Natchez Trace."

"Has he ever gone missing before?"

"No."

"Have you and your husband recently had a disagreement?"

"No."

"Has your husband recently had a run-in with anyone who might want to hurt him?"

"N—wait! Wednesday, while at work, he had a run-in with a couple of guys on his mail route. They shot at him. The Columbia Police have a report about it," she said.

Her mind began to race. Could those men somehow have found Daniel and done something to him? Her whole body began to shake.

"Don't worry!" Snell jumped in. "Most likely those men had nothing to do with your husband's disappearance. They probably had car trouble last night, then didn't have any way to get in touch with you. You said their cell phones went straight to voicemail? Probably because the batteries were dead. We'll get someone out there to take a look around. We'll find them for you."

"I hope you're right," Emily replied.

Deputy Snell got up from the table and handed Emily one of his business cards. "Please give me a call if he shows up," he stated and walked out the door.

Emily wasn't about to hang around all day, hoping the sheriff's department would find Daniel safe and sound. She decided to go looking for him on her own. So she took a quick shower and put on fresh clothes. She dressed for the hike she intended to make. She wore a T-shirt and jeans, her Timberland boots, and a light windbreaker, then put on her Atlanta Braves baseball cap. She also packed a small backpack—some food for the day, water, and a first aid kit. She also added a hunting knife, compass, and a butane lighter to the kit. At the last minute, she contacted the ranger station to see if they had any information about the two missing men. She Googled Natchez Trace Ranger Station, Tennessee. After clicking three different links, she found the phone number she hoped for. She dialed it and waited. After four rings, a young lady answered. "Ranger station. How can I help you?"

Emily replied, "Hi, my name is Emily Lane and my husband and a friend of his went trail riding yesterday on the trace and I haven't heard from them since. Have you had any reports up around the Shady Grove area about anyone getting hurt or anything like that?"

The young lady answered, "No, ma'am. But Ranger Douglas just began his patrol about fifteen minutes ago. So he probably hasn't made it out that far yet."

Emily instructed, "Well, I'm going out there to see if I can find them. Can you have the ranger call me, please?"

"Yes, ma'am," the young lady replied. "Can I get your number, please?"

Emily recited her phone number to her, then hung up the phone. Emily grabbed the backpack and then looked around to see what else she might need. She decided there wasn't anything else. As she walked into the garage to get into her car, she balked, then moved over to Daniel's truck and got into it instead. She started it up and backed out of the garage, then drove down the chert driveway and made a right turn. She drove down to Highway 412, made a right turn, and headed for the Trace. Five minutes into her drive, her phone rang. She checked the number. It was local but not from her contact list. She decided to answer.

"Hello?"

"Ms. Lane?" a man's voice asked.

"Yes, this is Emily Lane," she answered.

"Ms. Lane, this here's Ranger Matthew Douglas. I'm callin', you bout yur missin' husbun'."

Emily noticed his strong Tennessee accent. She thought He must be from Lawrence County.

"Yes, Ranger Douglas. Thank you so much for calling me."

He replied, "Yes, ma'am. I'm down here to the parkin' lot at Shady Grove and thar's a truck and horse trailer parked rat cheer, but thar ain't nobody here."

Emily spoke, "Ranger, would you mind waiting for me, please? I'm on my way. I should be there in about twenty minutes."

Ranger Douglas replied, "Naw ma'am. I don't mind a bit. I'm a gonna call it in to the station and see if I caint get us some help out here ta figger out whut happen to 'um."

"Thank you!" Emily replied. "I'll be there soon."

Emily sped up going down Highway 412. When she reached the entrance to the Trace, she knew she would have to be careful of her speed. The speed limit was 50 and strictly enforced, but she decided to fudge a little bit and did fifty-seven down the highway. Fifteen minutes later, she pulled into the parking lot at Shady Grove and found two ranger cruisers and Jimmy's pickup truck and trailer. She pulled in, parked next to the pickup, and got out to meet the two rangers.

"Hi, I'm Emily Lane," she said.

"Yessum," Ranger Douglas replied. "I thought ya might be. I'm Matthew Douglas, and this here's Tommy Brown. He's here ta give us a hand." Ranger Douglas was a short, stocky man. Emily measured him to be about 5'6"—a good four inches shorter than she was. He weighed at least 225 pounds. Ranger Brown, on the other hand, was at least 6 feet tall and built like a bean pole—straight and narrow.

"Well, what do you think?" Emily asked the two men.

"Well, we found some horseshoe tracks." Ranger Douglas answered. "It didn't rain none las' nite. So we art to be able ta foller them rat to where them two fellers ended up."

"Sounds good," Emily replied. "Let's see where they lead." Emily grabbed her backpack from the truck and mounted it to her back.

"Come prepared, did ya?" Ranger Douglas asked.

"Always!" she said.

The trio walked out into the trees, following the tracks along the trail that moved away from the parking lot. The tracks were distinct as the ground here was soft. Emily could see two sets of horse tracks and one set of dog tracks leading away from the parking area. There weren't any tracks going back to the lot. After half an hour of walking, they came to the bluff that overlooked the Duck River. The tracks turned back east, to their left. Emily carefully glanced over the bluff's edge just to make sure there wasn't anyone lying at the bottom. There wasn't. At least, not as far as she could tell. They eventually walked beneath the Trace Highway, moving along the river's edge but slightly moving away from it. They had been walking for about an hour now. Ranger Douglas was beginning to show some fatigue. Sweat was running down his face, and his shirt was wet. His breathing became labored.

"You, all right?" she asked, looking at Ranger Douglas.

"Yeah, I think I must've eat too many taters last nite. It's ketchin up with me," he replied.

"Let's take a little break," Emily said.

She pointed to a fallen tree nearby and motioned for the ranger to have a seat. He did. She removed the backpack and rummaged through it until she found three water bottles. She handed one to each ranger, opened the third, and took a sip. Ranger Brown spoke for the first time.

"You and your husband come out here a lot, do ya?"

"About 2 or 3 times a year," she replied. "We love it out here. The history intrigues Daniel. He was a history major in college. He also had ancestors that settled somewhere east of here. At least he thinks they did. He had a hand-written book from his grandmother, that talks about a man named William Lane who was killed in 1808 by Indians somewhere east of here. Nobody knows what happened to his wife, Sarah. She just disappeared, I guess."

"Where'd ja meet yer husband?" Ranger Brown asked.

"At college," She stated. "We attended Lipscomb University. He studied history while I studied nursing. Are you married, Mr. Brown?"

"No, I ain't," he answered.

"Why not?" she returned.

"I caint much talk to women," he said. "They kinda scare me."

"Well, you're talking to me. I'm a woman."

"Yessum, but yor marry't and I ain't tryin to ask you out on no date," he replied.

Emily nodded and gave him a slight smile. She couldn't help but think, "*This is a gentle man. He just lacks confidence when it comes to women. I bet he'd make someone a fine husband if they would take the time to get to know him.*"

Emily stood up and asked, "Are we ready, gentlemen?" The men also stood; only Ranger Douglas wobbled a little as he stood. Emily looked at him and suggested, "Mr. Douglas, you don't look so good. Why don't you let the two of us continue while you wait here?"

"Tell you what ma'am," he replied. "I believe I'll just do that. After I rest a spell, I'll make my way back up there to the Gordon House and see if I caint ketch a ride back to my car. Then I'll meet you two back at the Gordon House when yer done."

The three of them had settled in the open field behind the Gordon House exhibit. At this point, the house was about 200 yards from them.

"That sounds good," Emily replied. "Please don't overdo it."

Emily put the backpack on, and she and Ranger Brown started following the tracks that seemed to make a diagonal trail through the field moving east of the Gordon House. Halfway through the field, Emily glanced back to see if she could spot Ranger Douglas. He had left his resting place and was moving away from them toward the Gordon House. The path that she and Ranger Brown followed was easy enough to follow. The tracks were still there, but not as precise. But, the tall golden sage grass they trudged through had a parting through it. Evidence shows that large animals, in this case, two horses, had cut their way through, making it easy for Emily to follow. She and the ranger walked in silence. It was nice, she thought, to not be in constant conversation about nothing. At work, there was always a constant conversation about absolutely nothing. At least, nothing that really interested her. She found it exhausting at times. That's why she liked being outdoors, whether it was on their little farm in Hampshire or out here on the Trace. It was peaceful. No need for discussion only for the sake of having a discussion.

After about fifteen minutes, they came within forty yards of the field's edge. Emily looked down and noticed a change in the tracks. "Do you see that?" she asked the ranger.

"Yessum," he said. "Looks like one of the riders took off from here at a gallop. The other one is continuing at a walk."

They noticed that the second rider, too, began to gallop a little farther up. They were right at the edge of the trees surrounding the field. A slight notch in the trees created a path that was not easily seen.

"This ain't the normal trail, ma'am," Ranger Brown stated. "The regler trail runs own down south, about fifty yards from here."

The two of them walked slowly, following the tracks into the trees. After about ten yards, the tracks ended. Nothing. No dog tracks. No horse tracks. No footprints of any kind. The soil here was sandy. Emily took two large steps past where the tracks had ended, then turned back to look at her footprints.

"You see that?" she asked. "Where are the horse tracks? They aren't moving farther into the trees. They aren't going north or south! Where are they? My footprints are as clear as day."

"Yessum," the ranger added. "It's like both riders just disappeared!"

Daniel! she thought to herself. *Where are you?*

CHAPTER 4

After thirty minutes of rummaging and looking around for clues, Ranger Brown decided to call it.

"Ma'am, I think we've done all we can right now. We best be gettin' back to check on Matthew."

"Alright, Mr. Brown," she said.

"Call me Tommy, ma'am."

"Alright," she said. "You call me, Emily."

The two of them walked back through the open field of sage grass, but instead of following the trail back to the river, they made a sharp right turn and headed for the Gordon House. There they found Ranger Douglas sitting in his patrol car, waiting for them. As she approached his car, Emily could see that he was on his cell phone. When she got closer, he finished his call and got out of the vehicle.

"Ms. Lane," he said. "I just got off the phone with the Maury County Sheriff's Office. They were callin to check to see if anything turned up bout yor husband. Did jall find anythang?"

"No!" She sighed. "We followed the trail of tracks right into the tree line at the other side of that field. The tracks just suddenly ended. The ground was still soft and should have revealed which direction they took. But they just ended."

Ranger Douglas looked at Tommy for acknowledgment, and Tommy nodded to him. "Well, I'll be!" Matthew sighed. Then he responded, "Me and Tommy here will write up the report of what happened t'day and call the sheriff's office and let'm know. Is there anything else we can do fer ya?"

"No, Mr. Douglas," she replied. "Just get me back to my truck, please."

"We'll do, ma'am."

They all piled into the patrol unit and rode in silence for three minutes back to Shady Grove. As they pulled into the parking lot, Emily announced, "Thank you so much, gentlemen!"

"Sorry, we couldn't be more help, ma'am," Ranger Douglas replied. "We'll do whatever we can to find yor husband and his friend."

Emily and Tommy got out of the patrol car and moved over to their vehicles as Ranger Douglas pulled away and headed back south down the Natchez Trace Parkway.

"Tommy Brown, you were a big help to me today," she announced.

"Shore thang, ma'am... I mean Em'ly."

Emily smiled and looked at him in the eyes. "Would you mind if we share phone numbers? I'd like to have someone to talk to about the situation. Maybe you could let me know from time to time what's going on with the investigation."

"I don't mind none," he said.

They exchanged phone numbers and Emily started to turn back toward her truck. But then asked, "What do I need to do about Jim's truck and trailer?"

"Just leave it with me. I'll stay here til someone from the sheriff's office shows up to process it. They might even call in TBI," he said.

Emily nodded with understanding, then reached out her right hand to shake his. He obliged and took her hand, and she grabbed his with both of her own. "Thank you so much!" she said, looking into his eyes again. Tommy felt the warmth of her touch, and he looked at the ground away from her eyes and felt his face flush with embarrassment. Emily released his hand, then turned and got into her truck. As she drove from the parking lot and turned south onto the parkway, she still felt worried and concerned for Daniel and Jimmy. But she also felt a sense of warmth in knowing she had made a new friend today—a friend she felt she could trust with her deepest, darkest secrets.

When she left the parkway and drove back onto Highway 412, her cell phone came to life. Ting, ting, ting, ting. Emily evidently had not been in reach of cell towers while on the Trace. When she returned to the highway, her phone began to receive a signal again. She continued to drive for a while, ignoring the phone. She wasn't about to check it while driving. She had seen too many accident victims come into the hospital because of texting and driving. She also knew the cell phone signal would be spotty throughout her drive to Hampshire. She chose to wait the ten minutes it would take to get there. Once in Hampshire, she pulled into a parking space on the right side of the highway, in front of the Men's Club. It was the first of a series of storefronts lined the highway in Hampshire. Most of the stores had been abandoned at one time or another in this sleepy little community. But the Men's Club lived on and on. It was just an old store where the local old-timers used to get together, smoke their big stinky cigars or cigarettes, and "shoot the bull." There was less bullshooting and more gossiping than anything else.

From her parking space, Emily checked her phone. Three missed calls and seven text messages. All from her Aunt Linda. Linda Crockett was a short heavyset woman who wore her silver hair in a short "pixie" cut for as long as Emily could remember. She had been a sister to Emily's mom, who had died five years ago of breast cancer. Linda was sixty-five years old, had never been married, and retired from teaching school in the Lawrence County school system. She was outspoken, gossipy, and a busybody. But she was Emily's aunt, so she tolerated her as best she could. Linda was also the caretaker of Emily's most favorite person in the world, her grandfather. Grandpa Bill as she called him, or "Wild Bill" as he had been known in Lawrence County, was eighty-five years old. He was weak in body, but his mind was as sharp as a butcher's knife.

William "Wild Bill" Crockett was a rambunctious, opinionated man in his younger years. He loved to tell stories, some of which were true, and play practical jokes on the people he was close to. Many people in the community who hadn't known him well were uncomfortable with his wild manners. Those who knew him well loved him dearly. He had made his money in real estate. He was never rich, but he made enough to live comfortably, even in his later years. He was generous. He was always slipping someone in need, a twenty-dollar bill into their hand during a routine handshake. During the holiday season, he could be seen in the local Walmart, handing out one-hundred dollar bills to young struggling families trying to shop for gifts they couldn't afford. But as wild as he was in his storytelling and practical jokes, he never made a big deal about his giving to others. Grandpa Bill held a special place in Emily's heart. He always treated her special. He never spoiled her. He just spent as much time with her as he was allowed. He made sure she knew she was loved.

Emily found Aunt Linda's number on her cell and dialed it. A few seconds later, "Em'ly!" she heard. "Where you been? I've been tryin to reach you all mornin'."

"I've been out looking for Daniel," Emily replied. "He's been missing for a day and a half."

"Missing?" Linda questioned. "Well, where is he?"

Exasperated, Emily replied, "I don't know where he is. If I knew, he wouldn't be missing."

"Well!" Linda responded. "Never mind."

"What did you want?" Emily asked.

"It's your grandpa," Linda said. "He's been askin' for you all mornin'. Says he has to see ya right away."

"Why?" Emily asked.

"He won't say," responded Linda. "He's been demandin' ev'ry tin minutes for me to call you. He's getting on my last nerve, I tell ya!"

Emily heard a rumbling in the background.

"Yes," Linda said to someone other than Emily. "She wants to know what this is about," she continued to the voice.

More rumbling.

"Em'ly?" Linda continued. "He says you gotta come today. It's very important."

Emily thought deeply for a moment while biting her lower lip. Her eyes cocked to the right as she wondered, What in the world, could be so important?

"Okay, Aunt Linda!" she announced. "Tell Grandpa Bill I'm on my way."

Emily decided she was hungry. She got out of the truck and walked across the street to Whiteside's Market. She went inside and ordered a fried baloney and hoop cheese sandwich with a bottle of water. Five minutes later, she was back in the truck and on her way. She drove about one hundred feet before turning right onto Highway 166, heading south. She drove the five miles of road that wound around up and down hills while eating her sandwich. Ten minutes later, she turned right onto the Highway 43 Bypass. She would be in Lawrenceburg in about thirty minutes. She tried to concentrate on her driving, but it was difficult. All she wanted to think about was Daniel. What happened to him? Where is he now? Why was there no trace of him at the edge of the woods?

When she arrived in Lawrenceburg, she continued down the four-lane highway until she turned right onto Highway 64. Just a short distance down the road on the right was the entrance to the David Crockett State Park. Less than half a mile on the left was Grandpa Bill's house. She turned into the driveway and parked behind an old blue Mercury Sable - Aunt Linda's car. She got out of the truck and walked into the house and announced, "I'm here!"

She heard Linda's voice, "We're in the study."

Emily walked straight ahead to the back of the house and then entered her grandfather's office. There he was, Wild Bill Crockett, sitting behind his desk. As she entered the study, she saw his eyes light up and a huge smile covered his face. "Hi, Grandpa!" she greeted him. She walked over to him and lightly kissed him on his smooth cheek. The only part of his face that wasn't covered in wrinkles.

"Hey, sweetie," he responded with his raspy gravelly voice—a voice he developed over the years from smoking a pipe. When he spoke, it was difficult for most people to understand him because it seemed his tongue had grown too big for his mouth. But Emily understood him. His eyes left Emily and fixed on Linda. He pointed at the door and gruffly said, "Go!"

Linda took a deep breath, released it, and rolled her eyes a bit as she moved toward the door. She grabbed the doorknob as she went through and pulled the door shut behind her.

When Linda had left the room, Emily looked at her grandfather and asked, "Why did you need to see me?"

He jerked his right forefinger up to his lips to quiet her, then pointed at the door. "Make sure she's gone," he instructed.

Emily moved back to the door and quietly eased the door ajar. She could hear Linda moving around in the kitchen, banging pots and pans unhappily because she had been ejected from the secret meeting. "She's gone," Emily whispered.

Grandpa beckoned her back to his side and removed a small key from his vest pocket. "See that box up there?" he asked, pointing to a small wooden chest on the top shelf of his bookcase. "Grab it and bring it over here."

Emily did as he instructed but asked, "Where'd this come from?"

"Oh, it's always been here," he said. "I just kept moving it around from place to place to keep Nosey Nellie away from it."

By Nosey Nellie, he meant Aunt Linda. As she brought it down from the shelf, she observed that it was very old, very ornate. It was about the size of a cigar box. It was made of some sort of hardwood. Maybe hickory or walnut? It was decorated with inlay, maybe ivory or bone. She set it on the desk in front of her grandpa and waited for more instructions. Wild Bill took the tiny key and inserted it into the lock, then rotated it.

"This is why I called you here," he said. "Pull up that chair over next to me, here."

She sat down next to him and impatiently waited as he carefully swung open the lid to the box. He carefully and gently removed a piece of parchment from inside and unfolded it. "You know that we are direct descendants of Davy Crockett," he said.

"Yeah, but Grandpa, I thought that was just one of your tall tales you're always telling everybody," she responded.

He shook his head slowly and said, "No, honey. It's true. And, here's the proof." He turned over the parchment and showed Emily the back of the page. Six names and six dates were written on it. It was a list. It was her lineage. Each name and date had been written in a different handwriting and with a different pen. From the bottom of the list to the top, each entry faded more with age than the next. The list read:

David Crockett, born: 1786
Passed to his son, John Wesley Crockett, born 1807
Passed to his son, Robert Hamilton Crockett, born 1838
Passed to his son, John Wesley Crockett II, born 1861
Passed to his son, Robert Crowell Crockett, born 1880
Passed to his son, Stanley Finley Crockett, born 1902
Passed to his son William Wesley Crockett, born 1932

"We were all keepers of the Crockett family secret. This secret was known by only the men listed on this document. We have all been instructed to keep it safe along with this chest and its contents, until now." he stated.

"But, why now?" she asked. "What's so important about all this and why today?"

"That's for you to see for yourself," he answered. "The answers are on the other side of this document, and inside that little chest. First, I want you to read this document."

Emily carefully took the old piece of parchment and began to read it.

March 4, 1836

Dear J. W.

Well, son, it looks as if my time is running out. Me and my men are inside this little mission just outside of San Antone. We are surrounded by Santa Anna's army. There is a General Castrillon, who is in charge and seems to be a reasonable feller. He is gonna allow the women and children of our number to leave tomorrow, without harm. The rest of us will stay and fight. There is a Mrs. Baker who will be leaving tomorrow as her husband had already been kilt. She has agreed to take my letter and see that it gets delivered to you.

Son, what I am about to tell you is of great importance and should be kept secret. I have been entrusted by a young woman back in Tennessee to keep a small chest and hide it away. She called it a Time Capsule. I do not know what it means, but it was very important to her. She gave me a key and said the contents of the chest were not to be disturbed for 200 years. She said I should pass it down to one of my sons, and they should do the same when each man's life was near its end.

So, I am passing it on to you as my life will be over soon. The chest and the key are buried under the stump of that hickory tree that still stands next to the crick where we had the mill before it all got destroyed. They are wrapped in an old flour sack. Keep it safe and pass it on to one of your sons before you die. The contents are not to be disturbed by anyone until December 22, 2017. It is to be given to a woman in our family on that date. She is the only one who can open it.

Tell no one of this letter, son. Keep it safe with the chest. I am enclosing a second letter for you to give to Miss Lizzy. She can read it to all the family. Do not be uneasy about me. I am among friends. Farewell. David Crockett

Emily slowly lowered the parchment and stared at nothing.

"Well?" said Grandpa. "What do you think?"

"Grandpa, you're a direct descendant of Davy Crockett?" she asked.

"Emily, I've been telling you that for years!" he replied. "Did you think I was lying to you?"

"Well…" she replied. "You are known for being the best liar in Lawrence County. You've won the competition every year since I can remember."

He retorted, "Emily, I have never lied to you about anything. Never! Not even playfully. Everything that I have ever told you about the Crockett family, is true."

"Wow!" she said. "I've always wanted to believe it. Now, I've seen the proof."

"Well?" he asked.

"Well, what?" Emily returned.

"There's another letter in that box," he said. "No one has ever opened it. It's addressed to you."

"Me!" she exclaimed.

She reached into the box and carefully removed an envelope. It was yellowed from age, and on its back, it had been sealed with wax. An imprint had been stamped into the wax. Just three letters: ECL. She flipped the envelope over and saw it was addressed to Emily Crockett Lane and written in her own handwriting. She stared at it with astonishment; her mouth dropped open.

"What is this, Grandpa?" she asked. "Some sort of trick? How did this get in here? This envelope has my handwriting on it, and it has my seal. How did it get into this box?"

Grandpa reached out and took the letter to examine it. "I don't know, honey," he said. "That letter has been in that box for as long as I have had it. My father gave me that box to guard when I was forty-two years old, just before he died. As far as I know, that letter has been inside that box for almost two hundred years." He handed it back to Emily and asked, "Why don't you open it up and read it?"

Emily slowly reached to take the letter from his hand and deliberately and carefully opened the envelope. She slid a folded piece of paper from the envelope and carefully unfolded it. She again noticed that the handwriting looked like hers. But, how could it be? she thought. There are, I guess, some people who are very good at forgery. But how could it have ended up inside a small box almost two hundred years ago?

As she began to read the letter, her eyes began to narrow. Her brow furrowed. Her lips moved as she read intensely, but they never formed words. Then suddenly, her eyes widened with enlightenment. The answers to so many questions she had raised over the last thirty-six hours were now revealed. She looked at her grandpa straight in the eyes and announced, "Grandpa, I have something to tell you!"

CHAPTER 5

December 22, 1817: Daniel awoke abruptly from a light sleep. He was unable to get much rest during the night. His friend's body lay on the ground, five paces away, wrapped in Daniel's sleeping bag. Daniel had spent the night leaning against a large oak tree at the edge of the field where he had watched his friend die. He had been worried— concerned for his safety, and he was too cold to sleep well. He wore his windbreaker, but the weather had turned suddenly colder when he followed Jimbo into the forest—the forest that no longer existed. When he and Jimbo left home to come on this trail ride, the weather report called for low temperatures in the low 40s with a slight chance of rain during the evening hours. They had no reason to believe the temperature would be as cold as what he had experienced throughout the night. But he didn't dare to start a fire. He was afraid it would draw attention and the men who had killed his friend might return to finish him off as well.

As the morning sun began to rise above the edge of the trees, Daniel decided it was safe to head back to the truck. He thought *I'll get back there and try my cell phone again. Maybe I can find a signal good enough to call the police and report what had happened. Emily will be furious, too, when I call her.*

He got up from his position in front of the tree and moved over to where he had hobbled the bay stallion the night before. He removed the hobble, and the horse began pawing the ground as if to stretch out his joints. The horse snorted an approval, and Daniel rubbed his horse's face to acknowledge him. "Good, boy," he said. Then, he grabbed the saddle blanket and saddle, swung them onto the back of the horse, and cinched them down. All the while, Jake was still mourning at his master's side, whimpering. Daniel walked over to the dog and rubbed his head. "It's okay, Jake. We're gonna take him home."

Daniel picked up his fallen friend's body, wrapped it in the sleeping bag, lifted him precariously up, and draped him over the saddle. He took the rope from his saddle and tied the body on it to secure it to the horse and saddle. He grabbed the reins of the horse and then looked to the sky. The sun was topping the trees of the clearing where they had spent the night. He knew they had come in from the northwest side of the field. Looking around the edge of the field for signs that someone might be watching, he spoke to the dog and said, "Come on, Jake. Let's go home." Satisfied that the coast was clear, he led the way as the horse and dog followed.

When they had reached the edge of the field, Daniel looked into the trees. I know we came in from this direction, but it was an open field, he wondered. How could it have changed overnight? He felt he had little choice but to venture northwest into the forest. They would eventually have to find the Duck River or the Gordon House. Their progress was slow because there wasn't a clear trail. At least, none that he could see, anyway. They moved on at a snail's pace, stopping from time to time to check if anyone might be following them. After what must have been forty-five minutes of this routine, Daniel stopped and cocked his head to listen. "It's the Duck!" he said out loud. He could hear the waters of the river rushing southward in the distance. But something else too. He heard the voices of men yelling back and forth to one another. Jake heard it, too, and gave a little "woof."

"Come on, Jake!"

They moved more quickly, searching for the source of the voices. *Some-one is there.* he thought. *Maybe they have a cell phone with them that uses a different service provider. Maybe it has a signal so we can call the police.*

The trees began to thin, and suddenly, they were standing on a small bluff overlooking the Duck River. Daniel looked across the river, then looked to his left toward the south, then to his right. There they were. About fifty yards away were two men and what looked to be a log raft. Daniel moved toward them at a quickened pace. Finally, the trees opened into a clearing next to the river. Daniel stared with amazement at the two men. One was an old-timer, maybe sixty years old. He wore buckskin britches and tall leather boots. His blue shirt reminded Daniel of the shirts he used to see the Amish men wearing in Ethridge, Tennessee. He wore an old felt hat that slouched into his face from age. His face was wrinkled and brown except for the area covered in his long, gray-and-black, scraggly beard. The other man was younger. Daniel guessed maybe only eighteen or so. He was thin and tall, but his clothes were pretty much the same as the old man's, only his hat was newer and not so slouched.

"Howdy, friend!" the old man greeted Daniel. "Are you needin' to git cross the river?"

Daniel stood there with his mouth open, staring at a large log raft with four corner poles, which had a hole drilled through each one. A thick grass rope had been threaded through the holes. One on each side of the raft. Each rope was tied to a large tree on the north side of the river, then stretched over to the south side of the river, where they were tied off to trees on the south bank.

"It's a ferry!" Daniel proclaimed.

"Well, course it's a ferry," the old man retorted. "What'd ya spect?"

"It's so authentic looking!" Daniel exclaimed. "When did you guys restore it?"

"Restore?" asked the old man. "It don't need no restorin'. It's as solid t'day as the day it was built, fifteen year ago."

"Fifteen years?" Daniel questioned.

"Well, I'm through here all the time, and I haven't ever seen it! Is this the Gordon Ferry?"

"Yep, Cap'n Gordon hired me and young Tom there to run it fer him. Course, Tom's only been here bout a year.

My old pardner died last winter. My name's Gus!"

"Daniel," he replied. "Daniel Lane."

"Well, Dan'el. You look a mite confused. D'you fall off your horse or sum-um?"

Daniel just stared at nothing with his mouth open. Then Gus began again, "Say, that's a mighty fine-lookin' horse too. What's that you got on his back?"

"It's my friend, Jim," Daniel slowly mumbled. "He was killed yesterday, southeast of here."

"Injuns?" asked Gus.

"How did you know?" asked Daniel.

"Well, there ain't too many ways of dyin' round these parts. Fever, bar attack, or injuns. The most poplar way round here is injuns. There's a renegade band of Chickasaw that runs south of here. They don't much agree with the new ways Chief William Colbert is runnin' things these days. They like the old ways. There's a burial ground southeast of here, that they're mighty protective of."

Daniel closed his eyes and shook his head. "This is all just too weird. Can you tell me what the date is?"

Gus replied, "Well, I caint 'zactly tell the day. It's December. The year is 1817."

"Ha!" yelled Daniel. "I knew it. I'm just dreaming. Jimbo isn't really, dead. There are no Indians running around killing people. You're not here. This ferry isn't here. I'm not here. I'm asleep!"

Gus stared at Daniel and said, "Young feller, you need help. Let's go up to where the Gordon's are building their house. Miss Dolly will know what to do fer ya."

It was a fifteen-minute walk from the ferry to the campsite, where Captain John Gordon was having his house constructed. Daniel, Jake, and the horse followed Gus up the trail for the half-mile trek to the Gordon camp. When they arrived, Daniel saw that the house framing was near completion and the brick walls were just being started. There was also a small trading post just a little farther up the trail. To the west of the house was a campsite with one large tent and several other smaller tents, set up in two rows beside it. He thought the arrangement was typical of a military operation, and it seemed fitting that it would be done this way since John Gordon was indeed a captain in the Federal Army. He even supposed the tents were military-issued.

There were eight men currently working on the construction of the house in various ways. All but one of them was black. *Slaves?* Daniel wondered.

Gus walked up to the solitary white man and asked, "Titus, where's Miss Dolly?"

Titus was a tall, burly man with strong arms and intelligent eyes. "Oh, hey, Gus. She just headed up to the trading post a few minutes ago."

Gus turned to Daniel and said, "Why don't you wait here and rest a while. I'll go fetch Miss Dolly and bring her directly."

Without waiting for a response from Daniel, Gus turned and made his way to the trading post. Daniel looked around and found a log length that had been set up on end and was probably used for splitting firewood. He made his way over to the log and sat down to rest. Jake moved over to him, sat down between Daniel's legs, and allowed Daniel to rub his ears.

After a short while, Daniel noticed Gus and a woman walking back toward him. As they approached, Daniel stood to greet the woman. She walked right up to Daniel, taking in everything about him. She noticed the way he was dressed, the tack that his horse wore, and the blanket that his dead friend had been wrapped in were all wrong. There was something definitively different with this man. "I'm Dolly Gordon," she said.

"Daniel Lane, ma'am."

"Mr. Lane," she began. "I understand from Gus that you have had a rather difficult time of it, lately. What can I do to help you?"

"Well, Mrs. Gordon," he began, "I haven't eaten in over twenty-four hours. If you have a little something to spare, I would appreciate it. Then, maybe you could talk with me for a while and help me understand what has happened to me."

"I would be glad to do all of that, Mr. Lane." She turned to Titus and spoke, "Have one of the men take Mr. Lane's horse and unsaddle it. Tether the horse next to the corral so he can reach the water and have plenty of room to graze without being bothered by our horses. Then bring Mr. Lane's gear over to the camp where I'll be feeding him."

Then she turned to Gus and said, "You best be getting back to the ferry, Gus, before something happens to Tom. We don't want to bury two men in one day, now."

"Yessum," Gus responded, then turned and trotted back to the river.

"Come along, Mr. Lane," she said. "Let's get you squared away."

As they walked toward the camp, Dolly spoke to Daniel, "I hope you like stew, I started a big batch about two hours ago. It isn't quite done yet, but you should be able to get some nourishment out of it."

"Oh, yes, ma'am," he replied. "Anything would be just wonderful."

As they approached the fire pit, she pointed to one of two tables that sat side by side, close to the fire. "Have a seat, and we'll get you fixed right up."

Daniel sat at one of the tables as she had instructed. Each table was long enough to seat at least 10 people. Daniel tried to calculate in his head. He had seen eight slaves, one foreman, and two men at the ferry. There was bound to be at least one person at the trading post, and if he remembered correctly, the Gordons had eleven children. With Mr. and Mrs. Gordon, that meant twenty-five people probably ate at these tables at any given meal.

Jake came over and sat next to Daniel, then looked up at him. Daniel watched as Dolly approached the fire pit. There was an iron stand that stood to one side of the pit that stood about five feet tall. At the end of the iron stand was a boom arm that could be swung from side to side. At the end of the boom was a hook. Attached to a hook was a length of iron chain. At the end of the chain was another hook, and hanging from that hook was a large black iron cauldron. Daniel noticed the cauldron was not hanging directly over the fire but slightly to the side. He assumed that swinging the boom allowed them to regulate the temperature of the heat used to cook their food. Otherwise, food could never be simmered. It was full fire and burn it. Dolly reached over and caught the boom, then swung it toward her. Then, she grabbed a tin plate on the table and a big wooden ladle, which she used to scoop some of the stew onto the plate. She placed the plate of stew in front of Daniel and then handed him a large tin spoon. Then she reached over to another plate that was sitting on the table opposite Daniel. The plate was covered with a towel. She removed the towel to reveal six large cat-head biscuits.

"These were left from this morning," she said. "Help yourself."

Daniel grabbed one of the biscuits and dipped his spoon into the stew that was piled onto his plate. He tried very hard not to eat too quickly, but the stew was so tasty. And he was so hungry, he couldn't help himself.

Dolly offered, "I think I've got some meat scraps left from this morning for your dog if you like."

Daniel stopped his chewing for a moment, then cocked his head slightly in thought. Then he realized and said, "Oh, you mean Jake? Yeah, he probably would like that, but he's not my dog. He belongs... uh, he belonged to Jimbo."

Suddenly, Daniel wasn't starving anymore. He thought about his friend. He chewed more slowly now. With every swallow he made, his stomach filled with regret, remorse, and sorrow.

Dolly walked away temporarily, then came back to the table with a handful of meat scraps, mostly fat. She sat down on the opposite side of the table from Daniel, took one of the scraps, and held it out to Jake. Jake raised his nose, sniffing the air, then slowly moved toward Dolly and accepted the morsel of food. Jake barely chewed the meat, then swallowed it down, licking each side of his mouth— first the left side, then the right—in anticipation of the next bite. When the scraps were gone, Dolly began questioning Daniel. "Mr. Lane, you aren't from around here, are you?"

"No, I'm from southeast of here, over in Maury County." "I see you wear a ring. Are you married, then?"

"Yes, ma'am. My wife's name is Emily. We've been married for twelve years."

"Where is your wife, now?"

"She's back home. Probably worried sick about me. I was supposed to be home by dark, last night."

"Mr. Lane, I have a theory about you and how you ended up here. But I want to talk to you about it later. Are you finished eating?"

"Yes, ma'am."

"Good, then why don't we see about finding a place to bury your friend?"

Daniel looked startled and said, "Well, I had intended on taking him home after I notified the authorities about how he was killed."

Dolly put a hand to Daniel's arm to comfort him and said, "If my theory is right, then there is no authority here, who can help you. And you'll never get your friend back home."

Daniel was confused and in denial. He refused to believe that, somehow, he had entered a time portal of some kind that had sent him two hundred years back in time. If he, indeed, had traveled through time, when and where did it happen? As he and Dolly walked toward the corral where Jimbo's body lay, he recounted the events of yesterday in his mind. It didn't happen as they drove down the Trace Parkway. Or in the parking lot at Shady Grove. They were still traveling on asphalt and concrete at those points. So it had to have been somewhere on the trail ride.

They found Jimbo's body still wrapped in the sleeping bag, lying underneath a big cedar tree, away from the horses. Dolly called out to Titus, who was still supervising the work on the house and then beckoned him over to them. When he arrived, Dolly said, "Titus, let's get this man's friend a proper grave dug. We can put him over next to my Joshua."

"Yes, Mrs. Gordon," he replied. He then turned and called back to the house, "Nathan! Eli!" Then, he swung his arm around to motion for them to come.

The two men arrived, and then Titus said, "Grab a couple of shovels and a pickaxe. We got a grave to dig."

The two men scrambled, gathering up the tools they needed, and followed Titus as he led them to the spot behind the tented area of the camp, where Joshua was buried. Daniel asked, "Who was Joshua?"

Dolly responded, "He was my son. He died last winter of influenza."

"How old was he," Daniel asked.

"He was just thirteen. He was my youngest boy and my weakest. But, I loved him dearly."

"I'm sorry you lost him," Daniel consoled.

"Mr. Lane, I hope you'll excuse me for a while," she stated. "I've got a trading post that needs looking after, along with all the other deals we've got going on around here. You and I can talk more tonight, after supper." Without waiting for his response, she quickly walked away, heading for the trading post.

Daniel walked around the area, exploring, looking for clues as to whether or not this was really the Gordon place he had visited so many times in the past. Or was it the future? He spent some time watching the men as they worked on the house, making mortar for the bricks, laying the bricks, keeping everything just right. They were skilled, even artistic, at their craft. Two or three hours passed when Eli and Nathan returned from their dig site. Daniel saw them approach Titus who then turned and walked toward Daniel with the two men following.

"Mr. Lane," Titus said, "the grave is finished. If you're ready, they'll carry your friend's body over for you and help you bury him."

"Thank you, Titus," he answered. "Thank you all for your help."

Daniel followed Eli and Nathan over to Jimbo's body, under the cedar tree. The two men picked up the body and swung it up onto their shoulders, then carried it away with Daniel following. When they arrived at the gravesite, the two men lowered Jimbo's body onto a plank they had placed next to the open grave. Underneath the plank were two ropes. Each man grabbed both ends of a rope and then moved over to the open grave. Eli stood at the head and Nathan stood at the foot. They bent over and lifted the plank and the body with the ropes and slowly and carefully swung it over the open grave. Then, allowing the rope to slowly slip through their hands, they lowered the body into the grave. When it hit bottom, each man grabbed one end of the rope and pulled it out of the grave. Eli then asked, "Does ya won't ta say any words bafoe we covers him up?"

Daniel replied, "No, no I've already said my goodbyes to him. God will keep him safe, now."

As the two men filled the grave with the loose dirt that lay all around the grave, Daniel stared into the hole that held his friend. Jake came up and nudged his hand. He whimpered as more and more dirt filled the hole. Daniel's eyes began to water, and suddenly he thought of Emily and yearned so badly to be with her again.

They finished filling the grave just as the sun went down. The three men walked back to the campsite and found several people milling around performing various tasks in preparation for the evening meal. Daniel saw some people whom he had not seen earlier. There were a few black women and some younger white boys and girls ranging in age from fourteen to twenty. Mrs. Gordon and a young man walked up from the trading post to join them all. "Mr. Lane," she said, "did you get your friend buried all right?"

"Yes, ma'am," he replied. "Thank you for all of your help."

"Come and sit down, Mr. Lane," she said. "I'll introduce you to my family while we eat. Then, you and I can talk together after supper."

Mrs. Gordon took a seat at the head of one of the big tables and had Daniel sit to her right. Everyone else took their places. Titus, Gus, and Tom sat at the other end of the table while Mrs. Gordon's children filled in the spaces between all the spaces that the adults occupied. Then, Daniel noticed that the black men sat at the other table. The black women, on the other hand, did not sit. They would eat later. They served everyone else first.

After the food had been served, Mrs. Gordon said, "James, it is your turn."

A young man of about sixteen bowed his head and began to say a prayer as everyone else bowed their heads, too. As everyone started to eat their supper, Mrs. Gordon said, "Mr. Lane, these are my children. This is Amy the youngest. She's thirteen. Then Micah, he is fifteen, and James, who is seventeen. Then, there's Luke and Mark, the twins. They are eighteen, and Evan is nineteen. Last is John Jr., who is twenty-one. He helps me run the trading post. I have three older daughters. Two who are married and live in Nashville. My other daughter, Lucy, is visiting them right now. She's sixteen."

Daniel nodded to them all and said, "It's nice to meet you all."

The rest of the meal was spent chewing, poking fun at one another, challenges between some of the children, and talking about the day's events. After the meal, Mrs. Gordon said to Daniel, "Mr. Lane, would you care to walk with me, please?"

The two of them got up from the table, and he walked just half a pace behind her as they left the camp area. "All right, Mr. Lane," she began. "Well, Mr. Lane, something tells me you're just not from around here."

"What do you mean?" he asked.

"Well, I've not seen tack like yours on any horses around here. It looks like it might be Mexican or something. We had some people visit Nashville one time that rode on saddles similar to yours. They were from Spain. Your bridle isn't all leather. The reins are made of some kind of woven material. The rope you tied your friend onto the horse with, was not a grass rope. It was too hard. And the sack you had him wrapped up in, was some kind of material I've never seen except maybe on a fancy silk dress. Why don't you tell me what happened to you and your friend yesterday?"

Daniel was amazed at how observant she was. She would make a great detective. He told her of the day's events. How he and Jimbo had gone on their trail ride. How they had passed through her area along the Duck River and how they rode through her back pasture. How Jake had chased a deer into the trees, and Jimbo rode in after him. How he had heard Jimbo yell and then scream as Daniel rode into the trees after him. How he saw men dressed like Indians ride toward Jimbo and throw a lance into his chest, and then they stole his horse and rode away.

"Mr. Lane," she said. "You said you rode through my back pasture yesterday."

"Yes, ma'am," he replied.

"Mr. Lane, I don't have a back pasture. At least, not yet. We have plans to make a pasture back there, but not until after we finish building the house. Did you notice

anything... strange when you rode into the forest after your friend?"

Daniel thought momentarily and slowly said, "Everything went cold when I got about twenty feet into the forest. Then, this field appeared out of nowhere. That's where I saw the men kill Jimbo. He was on the other side of the field from me."

"Did you see anything... out of place before you entered that field?" she asked.

Daniel thought, and then his eyes widened with enlightenment. "Yeah! My horse sort of balked at one point. There was a kind of heat wave or strange waviness in front of us. Hoss didn't want to go through it, but when I heard Jimbo yell, I kicked him on through it. That's when things got cold."

Mrs. Gordon stood in silence for a moment, then spoke softly and slowly to him. "Mr. Lane, you need to be careful about speaking about what happened yesterday. The field you speak of is sacred ground to the Chickasaw. There is a burial mound in the middle of it. Most of the Chickasaw don't hold to a lot of the 'old ways' of thinking. Chief William has moved away from that lifestyle and become a bit of a capitalist. But there is a small band who still observe the old ways. They hate the white man and anyone who encroaches their sacred grounds. I can't tell you any more about what happened to you yesterday. I don't know anymore, and frankly, what I have told you just now, I have had no reason to believe any of it to be possible. Nothing more than Indian folklore. There is, however, someone you can speak with about it. But you must do it delicately. Do you understand?"

"Yes, ma'am," he replied. "Who is it?"

"There is a woman who runs a stand not far south of the Duck River. She's married to a Chickasaw man named David Colbert. He is a nephew to Chief William Colbert. He doesn't speak much English, but you can talk to Sarah and she can interpret. I recommend you head that way first thing tomorrow. If you find your answers, you might want to come back here and we'll talk again. I'll tell Gus to give you free passage over the ferry. I'm sure you can afford it, but I doubt any of your money would be good around here."

"Thanks!" said Daniel. "Thanks, for all your help."

December 23, 1817

The next morning, after breakfast, Daniel saddled up Hoss and rode toward the ferry with Jake trotting beside him. The morning air was cool—too cool for the light windbreaker he was wearing. But it was all he had with him. When they reached the ferry, Gus and Tom looked as if they had been waiting on him. "Come aboard," said Gus. "We'll get you across in a jiffy."

Daniel climbed down from his horse and led the horse onto the barge. Hoss had to be coaxed a little because the floorboards were a little uneven. He wasn't comfortable walking on them, especially while moving on top of the water. As Daniel led Hoss onto the barge, he was able to get a better look at its construction. The floorboards were made from split logs, with the split side facing up. They were laid side by side down the length of two long poles. From corner post to corner post, on each side of the barge was a side rail. Daniel hitched Hoss to one of these side rails, then stood next to him to soothe him and make him feel less nervous. Jake inspected the barge from end to end, pacing back and forth.

"Come here, Jake," Daniel commanded.

Jake moved over to Daniel's feet and looked up at him.

"Stay!" Daniel said, and Jake sat down next to him.

"Ready?" Gus asked.

"Ready," Daniel replied.

Gus stood on the left side of the barge, while Tom stood on the right side. They each gripped one of the ropes that ran through the corner post and began to pull the barge toward the other shore of the Duck. The water was swift but not too rough. The river's width was only about twenty-five yards across at this point, but much too deep and fast to cross on foot or horseback. Gus whistled the chorus of "No More Mr. Nice Guy" by Alice Cooper while he and Tom pulled on the ropes. *What is that tune?* Daniel thought to himself. When Gus realized that Daniel found the tune familiar, he changed his tune to "Jimmy Cracked Corn."

The water bucked the barge a bit as it rolled over a wave. Hoss snorted and rumbled while jerking his head a bit. "Easy, boy!" Daniel spoke to soothe him again.

Daniel placed his hand against the horse's muzzle and stroked the side of his head with his other hand. He looked down to find Jake still sitting beside him, panting with excitement. Periodically, water sloshed over the side of the barge, wetting Daniel's boots and pant legs. The water was cold—ice cold. As the barge moved into the shoreline, it stopped suddenly with a jolt as it hit the bank. Gus and Tom pulled hard against the ropes to bring the barge into its docking position for disembarkment.

"All ashore," called out Gus.

Daniel unhitched Hoss from the rail and led him off the barge onto dry land, with Jake following closely behind.

"Thanks, guys," Daniel said, turning back to look at Gus and Tom.

"D'you plan to be long?" Gus asked.

"Not sure," Daniel replied. "I'm headed up to the next stand to talk to a lady named Sarah. It could be a day or two."

"Well, it don't really matter," said Gus. "We'll be here awaitin', as long as it's before dark. That's when we shut her down."

Daniel gave them a short wave, then turned to the trail. He mounted Hoss and then kicked him into moving forward at a walk. The trail was well cut. In fact, it was much like a

dirt road he might find back home, except that it was not grated and smooth and narrow. Rain and the traffic of horses and carts had produced ruts and holes in the path that could make it a little bit of a rough ride. But it was better than riding through briars and heavy brush, which he had experienced while traveling through the forest on his way to the Gordon's place.

After five hours in the saddle, Daniel decided to dismount and take a break. Hoss took the opportunity to nibble on some of the sparse out-croppings of grass he could find near the trail. Daniel decided to check his saddlebags to see if maybe he had missed an energy bar or something he could nibble on himself. He raised the flap on one of the bags and reached in. Everything appeared to be as he had left it. First aid kit, flashlight, compass, his small Yeti thermos, and a short length of rope. He opened the thermos and tasted the contents. The coffee had been in there for over two days. It wasn't warm anymore. He spit it out, then emptied the thermos onto the ground. He poured a little water into the thermos and swished it around to rinse it out, then emptied it again. He put the thermos back into the bag, then closed the flap and moved around to the other side of the horse to check the other bag. He realized then that the bag was bulging a bit. "Hmm, what's this?" he said out loud. He slowly raised the flap and peeked into the bag. He found his hunting knife and his cell phone. But there was something else in the bag as well. Something of significant size. There was a poke sitting in the saddlebag. The poke was an old flour sack that had been twisted at the top to close it, then tied up with a piece of string. He also found a small leather pouch in the saddlebag. He pulled them both out of the bag to examine them more closely. First, he untied the string from the top of the poke.

Inside he found six biscuits and about a pound of jerky. "Probably deer meat," he said aloud. He decided to eat one of the biscuits and a little of the jerky, but not too much. He realized that things were not like his days back home had been. He couldn't just pull into a Fast Stop and order a full meal, fill up his gas tank, and then pay for it all with his debit card. Money and supplies would be sparse now. He would need to be careful with both. He packed the rest of the food back into the poke and put it in the saddlebag. He then opened the leather pouch. He poured the contents of the pouch into his left hand. In his hand jingled several silver coins. Some were silver dollars; others were smaller coins. In total, he found $5.25. "Thank you... Mrs. Gordon," he said.

Satisfied that Hoss had eaten a sufficient amount of grass, he decided it was time to be on their way. He put the coins back into the pouch and put it in his saddlebag. Before mounting back into the saddle, he decided it might be a good idea to keep his hunting knife handy. The knife was in a leather sheath, which had two slots cut in the back. He unfastened his belt and slid it out of two of the belt loops on his jeans, then threaded the belt through the sheath and ran the belt back through the loops. He then mounted Hoss, and they moved down the trail toward their destination.

Daniel had no idea how far he would have to travel to find the stand. He only knew that the exhibit on the Natchez Trace Parkway was a short drive from it to the Gordon House. However, the exhibit states that the stand's actual location was unknown. So, he would have to follow the trail until it led him to his destination. He knew that it was typically a day's ride from one stand to the next. He quickly found this was not the case with the distance from the Gordon House to Sheboss Stand. After another thirty minutes, the trail opened up a bit into an open area of cleared land about five acres in size. On the left side of the trail stood a small cabin. He had never seen one like it in person. But he had seen pictures of cabins like it. It was two structures about twelve feet square that were separated but joined together with an open area, which most people referred to as a dogtrot. The cover over the structures was one continuous roof that provided a shaded area for the dogtrot. Not far from the cabin was a small lean-to barn surrounded by a corral made of split logs. There were two horses mingling around in the corral, and a man wearing buckskin clothing was with them. Just as Daniel rode over to the corral to say hello, he saw that the man was Native American. He was not too tall, about 5'10", Daniel thought. His hair was black and shoulder length, but there were some gray hairs mixed in. Daniel thought him to be about forty-five years old. The man leaned over and crawled through the second and third rails of the corral fence, then walked toward Daniel. Daniel opened his mouth to speak when the man raised his right arm and pointed toward the cabin. "She, boss," he said.

Daniel sat for a moment with his mouth standing ajar. He smiled with his eyes and replied, "Right."

Daniel looked toward the cabin and saw that a woman had stepped out of the cabin and was standing in the dogtrot, looking at him. Daniel turned back to the man and nodded. He dismounted his horse and tied him to a hitching rail beside the corral. He removed his saddlebags and draped them over his right shoulder, then proceeded toward the cabin. As he approached, the woman said, "Howdy, you lookin' for a place to stay the night?"

Daniel saw the woman was about thirty years old. She wore a homespun dress with long sleeves, and her mousy brown hair was tied up on top of her head. She was slimly built, but Daniel knew she was strong for her size.

"Yes, ma'am," Daniel replied. "At least for the night."

The woman said, "Well, you and your dog can sleep in the cabin over here. That'll be four bits and includes your meals. We'll put your horse up and feed him for another four, so that'll be a dollar a night."

"Sounds good," Daniel responded.

He reached into his saddlebags without removing them from his shoulder. He dug around until he found the leather pouch and fished it out. He sorted through the coins without emptying them from the pouch and found a silver dollar, then handed it over to her.

The woman smiled and said, "Thanks! My name's Sarah Colbert, and that there's my husband, David," indicating the man at the corral. "Welcome to Sheboss."

"Thank you," Daniel replied. "My name is Daniel... Daniel Lane."

"Huh!" she said and looked at him a little puzzled. "Well, I can see from your duds, you ain't from around here. Where you from?"

"I live in Maury County, just outside of Columbia," he answered.

"Is that how folks dress in Columbia?" she asked.

"Well, sometimes," Daniel said.

"Well, that shirt you're wearing can't be very warm. What's it made of? Silk? Satin?"

"I don't know what it's made of," said Daniel. "But you're right. It isn't very warm. It
does help keep that cold wind from biting so hard, though."

Sarah led him into the dogtrot and asked, "Have you eaten today?"

"Well, I had breakfast up at the Gordon place this morning."

"Well, how 'bout a piece of apple pie and some coffee to hold you over 'til supper?" she asked.

"That sounds wonderful," Daniel replied.

"Well, have a seat right there, and I'll be right back." She motioned him to a table and two long benches placed inside the dogtrot. Daniel removed the saddlebags from his shoulder and set them on the bench next to him as he sat down.

As Sarah worked, getting together his pie and coffee, Daniel could see inside the cabin because she had left the door open. It was pretty much what he had expected. Sparsely furnished, all with handcrafted furniture. A feather tick bed sat in the far corner, while two rocking chairs rested near the front of the cabin. A small table sat between the two rockers and held an oil lamp on top of it. A rock fireplace was built at the far side of the cabin. There wasn't a stove, so she must have cooked in the fireplace. There was a table against the wall next to the fireplace, where the prep work was done when she cooked.

She soon presented Daniel with a tin plate containing an extra large piece of pie. Then, set a tin coffee cup in front of him and filled it with black liquid. Daniel was sure it would be strong, but he looked forward to the hot sensation as it ran down his throat. Sarah sat at the table across from him and offered, "There's honey in that jar right there if you like your coffee sweet."

"No, thanks! I like it black."

As Daniel enjoyed the pie and coffee, Sarah began to question him. "Did I hear you say your name was Lane?"

"Yes, ma'am. Daniel Lane," he answered.

"Did your folks come from North Carolina?"

Daniel replied, "Well, I think we had some distant relatives who were from North Carolina, and they eventually moved into East Tennessee. My father had some notes that were given to him by his father that even talked about a relative who was taking his family into East Tennessee that was killed in 1808."

Sarah furrowed her brow and said, "Really. What was his name and how was he killed?"

Daniel thought for a moment and said, "I think his name was William Lane, and he was killed by r—"

"Renegade Indians!" she finished for him.

Daniel nearly choked on the pie he was chewing. He looked at her, confused. "Did you know him?" he asked.

"William Lane was my late husband. We left Raleigh in 1808, headed for Nashville, where we intended to open a dry goods store. We made it all the way through the mountains and through the plateau just shy of Nashville when we were attacked by renegades. They were Chickasaw. But not like the one I married. They weren't tolerant of white people coming into their lands. Chief William Colbert is my David's uncle. He had his braves on patrol in that area, looking to keep the peace between his people and the white men. The renegades hit us, stole all of our supplies and horses, wounded me, and killed my husband. Before they could finish me off, they were run off by Chief William's soldiers. David was one of them. He was kind to me and nursed me back from death. Took me into their camp and introduced me to his uncle. When I told the chief about our perilous journey, he offered me a stand on the Natchez Trail, if I would marry David. I didn't know what else I could do. No one else was there offering me any help, so I took him up on his offer. I've been here ever since. I was twenty-two years old when that happened."

Daniel stared at her in shock. How did she survive? he thought. Then Daniel said, "I guess there is a good chance that you and I are related then."

Sarah looked at Daniel questioningly and asked, "Mr. Lane, I feel you are searching for something. What is it you are looking for?"

Daniel began, "I'm looking for answers to my questions. I'm hoping to find out how I ended up here, in this place, at this time."

"What do you mean?" she asked. "You rode up here on horseback. That's how you got here!"

Daniel slowly began, trying to keep his composure, "Dolly Gordon suspects something of me, and she told me that I might be able to get answers to my questions by talking to your husband. But she said I must be careful. Frankly, I don't know what I'm supposed to be careful about. You see, I was riding through this area two days ago with my friend. It was a ride that we had made together many times without incident. But two days ago, we ended up in a field that Mrs. Gordon told me was a burial ground for the Chickasaw. My friend was killed in that field. I buried him yesterday next to Mrs. Gordon's son. Do you know anything about that field?"

"It's called Tobi Okla," she said. "Sacred ground. I've never seen it. It is forbidden for whites to step foot there. Mr. Lane, tonight after supper, we'll talk to David and ask him about it. But we'll have to be careful. We can't let him know, right away, that you were at Tobi Okla."

That night, after supper, Sarah began to tell David about the conversation she and Daniel had earlier in the day. David sat and listened with little interest as she told how Daniel was possibly related to her late husband, William. David remained stoic through much of the conversation. From time to time, she would throw in a Chickasaw word when he didn't understand the English word she had used. She eventually got around to asking about Tobi Okla. "Why you want know 'bout Tobi Okla? Tobi Okla is keyu!"

"Forbidden," Sarah translated.

"I was near there, two days ago," Daniel said.

David's eyebrows raised. Daniel continued, "I am sorry. I did not know it was Tobi Okla. I was there accidentally. But I saw something that I have never seen before. I was hoping you could explain it to me." He looked at

Sarah now and said, "I saw a shimmering light that made a sort of gateway or doorway."

Now, Sarah raised her brows and slowly turned to David and asked, "Do you know Ittola Chuka?"

David sat silent for a while in thought. Then he began, "I have heard Ittola Chuka. I have never seen Ittola Chuka. Grandfathers tell of Ittola Chuka around fire. They tell story to warn. Stay away from Ittola Chuka. Story say, one time man come to our world through Ittola Chuka. Man was not from our world. Man was from another world. Man not live long, though. Ilbuk Losa find man, kill man."

Sarah translated, "Ilbuk Losa is the black hand. They are the renegades who guard Tobi Okla. They are also the ones who killed my late husband."

David continued, "When you say you see Ittola Chuka?"

"Two days ago," Daniel answered.

David stared in deep thought again and then said, "Two days ago was shila ah."

"Short day," Sarah translated.

"Short day?" Daniel asked.

"The shortest day of the year," she replied.

"Oh!" Daniel cried out. "The winter solstice. Yes, it was December twenty-first. I had forgotten all about that. Does that have any significance with Ittola Chuka?"

David nodded and said, "Hmm. Last time man walk through Ittola Chuka was faloha ah."

Daniel turned to Sarah questioningly, and she said, "Long day."

He then turned back to David and asked, "If the man your grandfathers spoke of passed through during faloha ah, and I passed through during shila ah, then it seems to reason that those are the two days of the year that Ittola Chuka opens." He looked at David and noticed him nod. Daniel's mind began to race. Would he be stuck in this century for another six months? Would he have to wait until next December? Or would he ever get back home to Emily?

CHAPTER 6

December 22, 2017: Emily looked at her grandpa straight in the eyes and announced, "Grandpa, I have something to tell you! Did Aunt Linda tell you that Daniel is missing?"

"Well, I don't know. She might have, but I have a knack of not listening to her."

Emily rolled her eyes a little and continued, "Well, he is. He went on a trail ride with one of his buddies yesterday on the Natchez Trace. They never came back home, so I called the police and got in touch with the park rangers on the Trace. The police weren't much help, but I met up with two rangers and they helped me search for him. We found the pickup truck and horse trailer, parked right where they had left them. We found their tracks and followed them until they came to an abrupt end. There wasn't any sign of them. It's like they just vanished."

Wild Bill asked, "You mean you didn't find him? You still don't know where he is?"

"Right!" said Emily. "At least I didn't until now. I now know where and when he is."

Puzzled, her grandpa asked, "What do you mean when?"

Emily handed him the letter and said, "It's all right here, in this letter."

Wild Bill took the letter from Emily's hand and started to read. "Sorry, honey. Would you mind reading it to me?"

Emily took back the letter and began to read it out loud.

Dear Emily;

What I am about to tell you will be disturbing and unbelievable. If today is December 22, 2017, then your husband, Daniel is missing. But don't be alarmed. He is safe. His friend, Jim, however, is dead. While on their trail ride on the Natchez Trace yesterday, they stumbled into an area known as the Shimmering. It is located at the edge of a Chickasaw burial site and is protected by a group called the Black Hand. Only, the Black Hand no longer exists. They did, however, exist two hundred years ago. That's where, or more precisely when, Daniel is now. The Shimmering is like a gateway between our world now and our world two hundred years ago. The gateway opens twice a year. During the winter solstice and during the summer solstice. As long as the sun is in the sky, the gateway remains open on those days.

Daniel is safe and searching for a way back home. You can expect to find him on June 21, 2018, at the location where you and the park ranger lost his trail on December 22nd. Be very careful going through the gateway. It's very dangerous. The Black Hand is patrolling that area every time the Shimmering occurs. Once you have entered the gateway, make a sharp left turn going west. This will allow you to enter through the gateway without entering the burial grounds. Daniel will find you there. Don't tell anyone about this except Grandpa and Ranger Brown. They are the only ones you can trust. Anyone who unknowingly enters that area on the solstice will end up dead.

I shouldn't give you too much information about the future. But know this: yours and Daniel's futures are in the past. Be prepared!

ECL

"ECL?" asked her grandpa.

"Emily Crockett Lane," she replied. "I wrote this, Grandpa. It's in my handwriting. I wrote this letter to myself almost two hundred years ago and gave it to Davy Crockett for safekeeping."

"Well, I'll be," replied her grandpa. "What are you gonna do?"

"Well, the letter says to be prepared," she said.

"Prepared for what?" he asked. "And what does that mean, 'your futures are in the past'?"

"I don't know what I'm supposed to be prepared for. And I don't know what the last part means either. It sounds pretty, evasive. I do think I need to be prepared for Daniel's return. I need to make plans. I think I should learn as much about the early 1800s as I can. That's typically Daniel's department. He was the history major in college."

"Hmm," said her grandpa, "maybe I know someone who can help with that. There's a man over at the state park that runs the David Crockett Museum. Our family has made donations of money and materials through the years to set up that museum. He is the expert on all things David Crockett."

"Can you call him for me?"

"Yeah, I'll give him a call, but he won't be there right now. It's too late in the evening. I'm sure he's gone home, now."

"Well, see if you can set it up for tomorrow afternoon," she said. "I have to get home right now, anyway. I've got animals to take care of." Emily said her goodbyes and left her grandpa and Linda to make the drive back to Hampshire.

Saturday, December 23, 2017

Emily woke up early out of habit. She missed Daniel and thought of him as she rose from the bed. But she was no longer worried. She knew he was safe. After a quick breakfast and a cup of coffee, Emily trekked up the hill to check on the livestock. She gathered eggs and checked on the mare. The goats and the hogs didn't need much looking after, so she just did a quick walk-through. Then she thought of Jinx, Jimmy Gleason's tomcat. She decided she should go over to Jimmy's and check on the cat. She walked back to the house and carried the eggs she had collected into the kitchen, where she washed them and stored them in the refrigerator. She fixed another cup of coffee and poured it into a stainless-steel carry cup. Then she walked into the garage and got into Daniel's truck and headed toward Jimmy's. She drove out of the driveway and turned left onto Biffle Lane, then made a left onto Cathey's Creek Rd. Near the end of Cathey's Creek, she turned left into Jimmy's driveway. Jimmy lived in a small single-wide trailer built in the 1970s. It was old, dirty, and rundown. The trailer was situated in the middle of a three-acre lot— three acres of junk. Old run-down cars, broken-down farm equipment, rusty fence posts, and water troughs turned up on their sides, which had rusted-out bottoms. The yard around the trailer appeared to have not been mowed for the last month of the summer mowing season.

Emily pulled up to the trailer and got out. She walked carefully, trying not to step on something that could bite or impale her. She walked up the steps of the wooden stoop, which stood in front of the door. The stoop rocked a bit as she stood on it. She checked the doorknob. It twisted in her hand, and the door opened easily. "Of course, it would be unlocked," she said aloud. "Who in their right mind would ever want to steal anything from here?"

A blast of hot, acrid air overwhelmed her as the door swung open. There was a strong smell of cat urine and feces, just aching to escape the enclosed space. "Poor, Jimmy," she said out loud. "He never was much of a housekeeper."

She hesitated to, but knew she needed to close the door to keep Jinx from escaping. She saw that at the end of what should have been the living area, an old CRT television from the 1980s was still on. An old Bob Ross painting show rerun was playing on PBS. Or at least, that's what she thought it was. The picture was so snowy it was difficult for her to make it out. She walked over and grabbed the rabbit ears antenna that rested on top of the TV and raised them. The picture cleared a little, but not much. They were fifty-five miles from Nashville. An old set of rabbit ears just wouldn't get you much this far out. She then reached to the front of the TV and pushed a button, and the picture disappeared.

Suddenly, a loud clang echoed behind her. She quickly turned to see Jinx staring at her while perched on the kitchen counter. He apparently had knocked a dirty pan to the floor to get her attention. "Jinxy! Hello, kitty!" She walked over to him and rubbed him between his ears and slowly moved down the length of his back. He arched his back to meet her hand movement. "Let's get you out of here." She knew that Jimmy owned a pet carrier because he used it to take Jinx to the vet when needed. She looked around the room, then walked into the spare bedroom, which didn't have a bed. It was just for storing stuff. After a little digging, she found the carrier underneath a pile of old newspapers. She looked for a place to put the newspapers but then shrugged her shoulders, grabbed the carrier, and pulled it out from under the newspapers as if performing a magic trick. Only the papers didn't stay in a stack. They scattered everywhere. "Good enough!" She returned to the kitchen and found Jinx still on the counter. She set the carrier on the counter next to him and opened it up. "Ok, kitty, you're coming with me." She picked him up and shoved him in through the opened door, then quickly shut and latched it. Jinx looked up at Emily with a concerned look in his eyes. "Don't worry. You're not going to the vet. I'll take you home with me."

Emily stowed the carrier and the cat in the back of the truck and got into the cab. She decided to check Jimmy's mailbox on the way out. There wasn't much in it. Just a couple of advertisements, but she grabbed them up and took them with her. She decided she needed to transfer his mail delivery to her address while he was away. She could do that online.

When she got back to her house, she walked into her kitchen and opened the pantry door. She took a can of tuna from the shelf and put it in the pocket of her jacket. She looked for a can opener and found it in the drawer where she kept her kitchen utensils, then put it in her pocket too. She walked back out to the truck and retrieved the carrier, then carried it up the hill to the barn. When she got to the barn, she put the carrier on the ground and opened it. Jinx was slow in coming out. He wasn't used to being outdoors. Emily took the can of tuna from her jacket pocket and opened it with the can opener, then placed it on a shelf in the barn, high enough up that the goats couldn't get to it. She showed Jinx where it was, then while he was eating the tuna, she made a getaway back to the house.

When Emily got back to the house, she noticed the message machine on their landline telephone was blinking. She walked over and pushed the play button. "*Beep*! You have three unheard messages. Message one: 'Hello, Daniel? This is Barbara. Just checking on you to see how you're doing. I've been trying to reach you on your cell. Give me a call back, please'. *Beep*! Message two: 'Mrs. Lane? This is Sergeant Hines with the Maury County Sheriff's Department. I just wanted to update you on the missing person's report you filed. Please call me back at 931-555-0100'. *Beep*! Message three: 'Mr. Lane? This is Sergeant Rawley with the Columbia Police Department. I just wanted to let you know that we caught two men that we believe to be the ones who shot at you. Please call me ASAP so we can set up a time for you to make a positive ID on them. 931-555-0800'. You have zero unheard messages."

Emily decided to call the sheriff's office first. Almost immediately after she dialed the number, someone answered. "Sheriff's office."

"Yes, this is Emily Lane. May I speak to Sergeant Hines, please?"

"Hold, please."

"Sergeant Hines, here."

"Sergeant, this is Emily Lane. I received your message just now. Do you know anything about my husband?"

"No, ma'am. I spoke with Ranger Matthew Douglas, and of course, you already know what they found because he said you were down there talking to him."

"Yes, sir. So, there isn't any new information?"

"No, ma'am. We've impounded the truck and trailer registered to James Robert Gleason. If you hear from him or your husband, please let us know. Otherwise, we'll keep the case open for now and keep an eye out for them."

"Thank you, sergeant. I will call if I hear from them."

She then called the Columbia Police Department.

"Police department."

"Hello, my name is Emily Lane. May I please speak with Sergeant Rawley?"

"Yes, ma'am. Hold please."

"Sergeant Rawley, speaking."

"Sergeant Rawley, this is Emily Lane. You were trying to reach my husband, Daniel about the men who shot at him?"

"Yes, ma'am. Is your husband around, I need to speak with, him."

"No, I'm sorry. He and a friend went on a trail ride on the twenty-first and never came back. I filed a missing person's report with the sheriff's office the following day, but they haven't found him yet."

"Oh, I'm sorry, Mrs. Lane. I hope he is all right. I'm sure we can make a case against these two individuals without his testimony, but it would be a much stronger case with your husband there to identify them. Please have him contact us if... uh, when he shows up."

"I'll do that, sergeant, and thank you."

The last call would be difficult. What would she say to Barbara, Daniel's supervisor?

"Sorry, he can't come to work on Monday. He's two hundred years away."

Emily dialed the number for the post office. "Columbia Post Office, Barbara speaking."

"Barbara, hi, it's Emily Lane."

"Hi, Emily. How's Daniel?"

"Well, I don't really know. He's missing."

"Missing? What do you mean missing?"

"Well, he and a friend went on a trail ride together the day after his accident to help relieve some stress. They never came back. The police found their vehicle, but no sign of them anywhere."

"Oh my! How terrible!"

"Barbara, I know he'll be back. I just don't know when. But will he have a job when he does?"

"Oh, sure! I'll put him on administrative leave for now. That will keep his route open until he comes back. I just hope he's okay, Emily."

"Me too! Thanks, for your help."

"Sure, thing! Just let me know if there is anything else I can do for you."

As she hung up the phone, something suddenly occurred to Emily. Daniel was stuck in 1817 and probably didn't know that the doorway home would be opening back up in June. He wouldn't know that he should meet her at the spot where he had disappeared. How could he know? The letter she had written to herself was written from the other side. If she ever saw Daniel again, it would be because she had crossed through the Shimmering into his new world. She decided that she would need to be prepared. She needed to gather supplies to help her make the trip through the Shimmering, and after she made it through. She needed to talk to her grandfather's friend, Henry Slater, the curator of the Davy Crockett Museum. It was Saturday, December 23rd. Would he be working today or taking a long weekend for Christmas break? She decided to call her grandpa.

"Hello?" said a voice over the phone.

"Aunt Linda? It's me, Emily."

"Oh, hey, Em'ly! I was just gettin' ready to call you. Your grandpa's needin' to talk to you uh-gin."

Emily heard her grandpa barking orders in the distance, but couldn't make out what he was saying. "She's own the phone, Daddy!"

Linda yelled back to him. "Hang own, Em'ly. He wonts to talk to ya."

After a few moments, a voice came on the phone, "Emily?"

"Hey, Grandpa!"

"Emily, I talked to Hank just a few minutes ago. He said the museum is closed today, but he'd meet you over there at 1 o'clock today to help you with anything he can."

Emily replied, "Grandpa, that's great, but how much did you tell him?"

Grandpa answered, "I didn't tell him squat! Only that he needed to give you anything you wanted that belonged to me. He's been holding a lot of artifacts and family heirlooms for me for years. They all belong to you now."

"Thanks, Grandpa. You've been a big help."

Grandpa spoke again, "Emily? Are you coming for Christmas this year?"

"No, I have to work Christmas day this year. Are you and Aunt Linda going to church tomorrow?"

He replied, "Well, if I can get up enough motivation, I guess I'll go."

Emily stated, "Well, if you'll go, I'll go with you."

"It's a deal!" he replied. "Meet us here at 10 o'clock, church starts at 10:30."

"Okay, I'll be there. See you, then."

Emily looked at the time display on her cell phone. It was 10:15. She had just enough time to shower, get dressed, and be on her way to Lawrence-burg. There, she would grab a bite to eat before she had to meet Henry Slater.

~~~~~~~~~~~~~~~~~~~

Emily drove the pickup truck into the parking lot of the Dairy Queen and parked. It was noon. She had plenty of time to grab a quick bite and make the short drive to the museum. She walked into the restaurant, which was somewhat busy. While standing in line, she decided on just an order of fries and a chocolate milkshake. She was a little nervous, and her anxiety was high in anticipation of meeting her grandpa's old friend for the first time. No sense in overdoing it with a full meal with her stomach churning the way it was. After placing her order, she walked into the dining area and found a place to sit. There were groups and families all around her, heavy into conversations about the day's events. Emily longed to have Daniel sitting across from her. She missed him so much she ached all over. An employee walked up to her and presented her with her order. Emily looked up and thanked the young woman as she set the food tray on the table.

"Yes, ma'am," she said. "Can I get you anything else?"

"No, thank you," Emily replied.

Emily slowly munched on the fries and sipped the shake while constantly checking her phone's time display. Occasionally, she would glance up to the TV screen, which hung on the wall in the dining area. There was an NFL game just starting—Colts versus Ravens. After eating only half of the fries, she decided it was time to go. Emily hated being late for anything. She felt it was downright rude for people to be late. She knew so many people who didn't share her philosophy on tardiness. It seemed that a whole new generation had formed that believed there was absolutely nothing wrong with being tardy and no reason for apologizing, should it occur. Emily tried her best to always be on time, if not early for all of her appointments.

She got back into the truck with her milkshake and pulled back onto the highway that would take her to David Crockett State Park. The museum was in the heart of the park. It would take ten to fifteen minutes at least to drive through the park's winding roads to reach her destination. She passed by the park headquarters, where she saw two patrol cars parked. A playground was set off to her right as she drove up a small hill. The road wound left past a camping area where several RVs were parked. As she came back down the little hill, she noticed a group of six deer grazing in the distance down to her left.

She came to a fork in the road. She took the right fork, although it really didn't matter because the road just made a loop. She eventually came to a small parking lot in front of an old log structure. There was only one other vehicle in the lot. It was a silver Nissan Sentra. Emily parked in the spot adjacent to the Sentra and got out of the truck. A short heavyset man with long silver hair that was tied back into a ponytail got out of the car and greeted her. He wore wire-rimmed glasses with round lenses that sat on the end of his nose. Although his hair was long in the back, he was completely bald on top. She couldn't decide who he was trying to mimic—John Lennon or Benjamin Franklin. He reached out with his right hand and said, "Emily?"

"Yes," she responded.

"I'm Hank Slater. It's so nice to meet you," he said with a smile.

"Thank you for meeting me on such short notice," Emily replied.

"Oh, not at all," he said. "Your grandfather speaks very highly of you, as he should. You just let me know what you need and consider it done. Have you ever been here before?"

"Yes, I have. My husband loves to come here."

"He couldn't come today?"

"No, he's out of town right now."

"Oh, I see. Well, come on in and let's see how I can help."

As they walked to the front door together, Emily noticed the old wooden water wheel on display just outside the structure. The wheel was a replica. It wasn't authentic to the Crockett family business. Davy Crockett had several business ventures, which his wife, Polly, looked after. One of those businesses was manufacturing gunpowder. They also operated a still to make whiskey, and she ran a trading post. As Hank unlocked and opened the door, he turned and saw a group of four people getting out of a car. Hank said when he saw them walking toward the building, "Go on in, Emily. I'll let them know we're closed."

As Emily stepped inside, Hank quickly walked toward the group and announced with a high-pitched squeal, "Sorry, folks! We're closed for the holiday. We're just here to do a little maintenance."

As Emily waited inside, she wandered through the exhibit hallway a little. She had seen it all before but never really paid attention to it. This was Daniel's domain. He would stand at each exhibit and read every word of every plaque as if he were memorizing them all. Daniel knew more about her family history than she did. She never really believed she was a direct descendant of the famous Davy Crockett. She thought it was a coincidence that they shared the same last name.

Hank entered the doorway, then turned and locked the doors. There was another locked door to his immediate right. Emily came back into view when she heard him enter. When he looked up and saw her, he said, "Come on in here," as he unlocked the door.

Emily walked into the room and looked around as Hank turned on the lights. She saw rows of shelves that reached toward the ceiling, storing various items. All of them, antique. There were areas set up on tables where relics were being cleaned and restored. There were drawers containing archeological tools for digging and cleaning— small picks and brushes of various sizes. At the far end of the room was a large door. The door had a dial and a handle. It was a safe. Not a safe, a vault. Emily glanced at Hank, and he pointed and said, "Inside that vault are all the items your grandfather brought to me for safekeeping over thirty years ago. He left strict instructions that everything was to remain in the vault until he said otherwise. If anything happened to him, I was given instructions to contact you and turn everything over to you. I have no idea of its contents, but I can tell you, it's a good thing you brought that truck. You're going to need it if your planning on emptying that vault."

CHAPTER 7

H ank Slater walked over to the vault and dialed the combination
lock. He then turned the handle, which released the lock, and
swung the door open. He reached inside and found a light switch, then
flipped it up to turn the lights on. Emily joined him at the doorway to
the vault and peered inside. She slowly panned her eyes around the room,
searching for clues about its contents. There were large wooden crates
stacked on top of each other. Four small wooden kegs were stacked in one
corner. There was an old steamer trunk pushed into another corner. Then,
lastly, a small wooden chest, very ornate, was placed conspicuously on a
shelf all by itself. Staring at the cache inside the vault, Emily asked, "Do
you have a hammer and a crowbar?"

Hank scurried back into the previous room and quickly returned with
both. "Let's open these wooden crates first," Emily said.

Hank walked over to the nearest crate, placed the flat end of the crowbar underneath the lid, and hit the other end of the crowbar with the
hammer. He pried off the lid, and the two of them peeked inside. Emily
raked aside the shredded packing material to find kitchen items. There
were tin spoons, forks and knives, tin plates, cast iron skillets, and Dutch
ovens—everything needed to set up an outdoor cooking area.

The two of them lifted the crate from the stack and placed it aside on
the floor. Hank then opened the next larger crate. This crate was long and
narrow, about six feet long and two feet wide. Inside were three Kentucky

long rifles, three tomahawks, and two flintlock pistols. Emily asked, "Do you see any ammo?"

Hank looked around and pointed to the four kegs in the corner of the room. "My guess is, those kegs contain lead shot and black powder."

They moved to the last of the wooden crates, large enough to hold a medium-sized animal. Inside the crate were farm implements. There were hoes, shovels, axes, picks, rakes, and a plow. They opened the steamer trunk and found various home items—oil lamps, small tools like hammers, a drawing knife, bit and brace, and other items Emily didn't readily recognize.

All that was left was the small chest. The chest was twelve inches long, eight inches wide, and about ten inches tall. It was hand-carved wood, fastened together with brass straps and hinges. There was a heavy lock on the front. Emily tried to remove it from the shelf, but it was much too heavy. Hank moved over to help, and the two of them lifted it onto the floor. It must have weighed thirty pounds. Emily looked around. She didn't see a key anywhere. She asked, "No key?"

Hank shrugged his shoulders and replied, "Not that I've seen."

"Well, let's get this loaded into the truck. I've got a pair of bolt cutters at home that will do the trick. Can you keep the rest of the stuff here for a while longer?"

Hank nodded. "It's been here for thirty years. It won't hurt for it to stay a bit longer."

Emily asked, "Can you help me carry this chest to the truck?"

"I'll do you one better," he replied. Hank stepped out of the vault, then returned after a short while, pushing a two-wheeled dolly. "This will save our backs," he stated.

The two of them loaded the chest onto the dolly. Emily looked around and found an old dusty towel that she draped over the chest. "No sense in advertising, huh?" she said.

Then, Emily took control of the dolly while Hank raised the chest to help her maintain the balance of it so she could roll it out of the vault. Once they had exited the vault, Hank secured the door. They moved together toward the parking lot, with Hank opening and closing doors as they came to them. He stopped momentarily to lock the outer doors of the museum in case new visitors showed up and tried to enter while they were loading the chest into Emily's truck. Luckily, no one showed as they loaded the chest into the back of the truck. They wrapped the towel around the chest, securing it with the weight of the chest so the wind would not blow it away as she made her way home. Emily raised the tailgate and secured it, then turned to say goodbye to Hank. He said, "I surely wouldn't mind knowing what you find in there if you don't mind sharing."

Emily responded, "And you deserve to know with all that you've done for my grandpa and me. When I come back to pick up the rest of the stuff, I'll tell you all about it."

She smiled, then turned away and got into the truck's cab. Then she waved to him as she pulled out of the parking lot.

~~~~~~~~~~~~~~~~~~~~

As Emily pulled into the driveway of their little farmhouse, she pushed the button for the garage door opener, then pulled into the garage slowly. As she parked, she noticed something on the back wall of the garage. Hanging, among other various power tools, was an electric angle grinder. "*Huh!*" she thought. "*I didn't know Daniel owned one of those.*"

When she got out of the truck, she walked over to the tool area and grabbed the grinder. Then she looked around, opening drawers, and found a pair of safety goggles and a pair of garden gloves. She walked to the back of the truck and lowered the tailgate. The towel was still somewhat in place. She removed the towel and dragged the chest onto the tailgate for easier access. She plugged the grinder into a wall socket, put on the gloves and goggles, and then worked on the lock. Sparks flew as the wheel whirled, sending tiny bits of rusty metal flying in all directions. It wasn't long before the lock lay in two pieces next to the chest on the tailgate. Emily laid the grinder aside on the tailgate, then stepped back a little to look around. She looked behind her, where the nearest neighbor lived. Their house was at least three hundred yards away. She couldn't see anyone stirring around. She listened for movement along the road in front of the house. Nothing. She stepped back into the garage, moved to the truck's cab, and hit the remote button to close the garage door. After the door closed, she moved back to the tailgate and stood in front of the chest. She closed her eyes, drew a deep breath, and then let it go. As she lifted the lid, the hinges fought against her pull. With a creek, the lid moaned but gave way to allow her to view its contents. Inside were ten leather pouches. She took out one of the pouches to examine it more closely. As she slowly opened the pouch to peak into it, the room suddenly went black. Emily's heart sank for a moment; then she realized that the timer had expired on the light of the garage door opener.

"Ugh!" she said out loud.

She walked over to the stoop leading to the house's door, reached up, and flipped on the light. She walked back over to the chest, opened the pouch again, and looked inside.

"Whoa!" she said in a soft voice. "What am I going to do with this?"

She dumped out the contents onto the tailgate and stared in awe as dozens of gold and silver coins spilled onto the tailgate. She counted the coins. Each was either a gold or silver dollar at face value. But these were minted in the late 1700s and early 1800s. They would certainly be worth more than face value. There were fifty coins in the pouch. "*That's fifty dollars!*" she thought. "*If each bag holds that much, then there's $500.*"

Her mind began to race. What would she do with it all? She couldn't walk into the bank and say, "*I'd like to deposit this, please.*" No, that wouldn't raise anyone's suspicions, would it? She couldn't even put it in a safety deposit box. What if an emergency happened and the bank just happened to be closed? How would she get her money back? She didn't have a safe in the house. Her grandmother used to keep mad money in a cookie jar on the top shelf of her pantry, but Emily didn't own a cookie jar. And if she did, it wouldn't be large enough to hold so much coinage. She finally settled on a solution, at least temporarily, until she could find a better solution. She carried the pouches into the mudroom that lay just inside the garage. She opened the door of her sixteen-cubic foot upright freezer. She took out several of the packages of pork that were stored there and then set them aside temporarily. She then put the pouches of coins into the freezer and covered them with the packs of pork to hide them. She admired her work and said, "Now that's what I call cold, hard cash. You might even say my assets are frozen." Then she chuckled and closed the door of the freezer.

****

December 24, 1817

Daniel awoke with a start. He heard Jake give a little "*woof*." Someone was moving outside their room. Daniel got out of bed and walked to the window in front of his room. The sun was barely peeking over the tops of the trees. A new day had begun. He walked over to the bureau that stood against the wall next to his bed and then poured water into the pan that had been provided. He washed his face. He now had three days' worth of beard. Daniel had never grown a beard. Emily liked him clean-shaven. He once tried to grow one, but she convinced him his beard was too sparse. That was ten years ago. He was barely a man then. His beard was coming in full bore now. He dried his face and hands, then pulled on his boots and donned his windbreaker before opening the door that led outside.

There, he found Sarah gathering a few sticks of firewood to take into the house.

"Morning!" she said with a smile.

"Good morning!" replied Daniel. "What day is it?"

"Well, it's Christmas Eve, December twenty-fourth."

Daniel looked at her quizzingly and said, "Yes, but what day of the week is it?"

"Oh!" she said. "It's Wednesday!"

Daniel thought for a moment. He began his journey with Jimbo on the twenty-first, which was Thursday. Today was the twenty-fourth, but here it's Wednesday. Back home, it would be Sunday. He and Emily would start their day together, preparing for church. They would walk to the barn together. Emily would milk the goat, while Daniel would gather the eggs and feed the other animals.

"Is there anything I can do to help this morning?" Daniel asked.

"You can bring in some of this wood for me," Sarah replied.

Daniel gathered several pieces of the split wood stacked against the cabin's outer wall, then followed Sarah inside. She showed Daniel where to stack the wood, then moved to a table and continued working on breakfast. There was a setup for cooking, much like Mrs. Gordon used, but it was only inside. The fire was built inside a fireplace. Over the top was a wrought iron rack where pots and pans could rest while cooking. A Dutch oven was on one side of the rack where Daniel supposed biscuits were baking. On the other end was a large black skillet where Sarah placed long bacon strips to fry.

"How do you like your bacon?" she asked.

"I like it cooked well, but not burned," Daniel answered. "Me too,"

Sarah said. "David likes his just barely cooked. He would eat it raw if I let him."

"What are your plans now that you know about Ittola Chuka?" Sarah asked.

"Well, I really don't know. I thought I would go back to the Gordon place and see if I might be able to work there for a while. Maybe help with the building of her new house. Aside from that, I don't know."

"Will you be leaving today?" she asked.

"Well, I guess so. I don't see any point in lingering here. I'd just be getting in the way."

"No, you wouldn't," Sarah corrected him. "I wish you would stay for at least another day. Tomorrow will be Christmas. David is going to see if he can kill us a turkey for Christmas Dinner. We'd love to have you stay as our guest. No charge. I wouldn't feel right charging you now that I know we're practically related."

Daniel looked at her and smiled a little, then said, "I'd like that. Only, I want to be of help. Put me to work so I don't feel so useless."

Sarah held out her hand to him and said, "That's a deal!"

After breakfast, Daniel approached David and said, "Sarah says you're going hunting today. May I go with you?"

David looked back at Daniel. With a slight nod and a short grunt, "Yes," he acknowledged Daniel's request. David gathered his gear, including his rifle and powder horn, and then they started toward the woods in search of a turkey. David glanced back and noticed Jake following behind them, so he suddenly stopped. "Dog not go."

"Why not?" asked Daniel.

"Dog bark. Scare birds."

Daniel replied, "Don't worry. He won't bark. He's trained to hunt. He's a retriever."

David furrowed his brow and asked, "Re-tree-ver?"

"Yes," said Daniel. "After you shoot the turkey, Jake will go and get it and bring it back to you."

"Hmph!" said David skeptically.

"Really!" said Daniel. "I'll tell you what. If Jake makes too much noise, I'll turn around and bring him back. Then you can finish the hunt by yourself."

David gave another "Hmph!" and then turned and continued searching the woods for their game.

They walked for what seemed to Daniel to be about thirty minutes. The trees were mostly bare of leaves, except for the cedars and firs that were sparsely spread across the landscape. Occasionally, a squirrel would run through the tops of the trees, leaping from limb to limb and from tree to tree like an acrobat. David led Daniel and Jake to a large, fallen hickory tree, where they settled in to wait for their prey. Once they were all set, David proceeded with his enticing calls of the turkey hen. He chirped, squeaked, squawked, chuck-chucked, and put them all together into a beautiful song that no Tom in his right mind could resist. His song echoed throughout the expanse of the forest as if they were sitting in an old country church with wooden floors and unpadded pews. The calls must have reverberated for miles.

Daniel leaned back against a tree while enjoying David's song as it rang out. Jake sat next to him, pricking up his ears every time David changed his tune's tempo or cadence. After thirty minutes or so, David stopped. He listened. Jake gave a slight snort as he stared into the distance. Daniel still couldn't hear anything of interest, but he could tell that David and Jake had heard it. David started his call again, but this time in shorter bursts, allowing short breaks for the turkey to reply.

Jake shuddered with anticipation as the voice of the Tom came closer, but Jake never made a sound. David noticed this, and he was mildly impressed. It took about fifteen minutes for the bird to enter the small clearing that lay directly in front of the hunters. While continuing his calls, David brought his rifle up to his shoulder, then cocked the hammer and aimed. David chirped, causing the turkey to cock his head and hold it still as if listening for something unfamiliar. David seized the opportunity and squeezed the trigger of his rifle. A shot rang out that echoed for miles. Birds and squirrels perched in the treetops suddenly burst into flight and

movement away from the men. Smoke billowed from the rifle barrel, making it impossible to see whether or not David's aim was true. Daniel's ears rang from the explosion of the muzzle-loaded rifle. His 3030 Remington back home had nothing on this noisemaker. It was more like a cannon blast at a Civil War Battle reenactment than a rifle shot.

Jake gave a little ruff and pulled against Daniel as he held on to Jake's collar. "Okay, Jake," he said. "Go get him!"

Jake leaped over the fallen tree, which had concealed them, then darted straight for the clearing where the turkey's body lay. The smoke was only slightly clearing now, as the two men saw Jake pounce on the bird, grabbing it by the neck. He then dragged the ten-pound turkey back to where they had all been hiding. David and Daniel hopped over the tree to meet Jake as he ran up to them. David was amazed and impressed when the dog laid the dead bird at his feet. Daniel, too, was impressed when he saw that the shot David made had decapitated the turkey. The two men stood together, smiling at one another. "That was a beautiful shot!" Daniel praised David.

David replied, "Good dog."

When they all returned to the cabin, Sarah greeted the trio from a distance with a wave and a smile. She was standing next to a cauldron over a fire that she had prepared. The cauldron was filled halfway with water, and it was steaming hot. David handed over the turkey to Sarah, and she said, "My, what a big one!"

She took a large knife and removed the bird's neck, all the way to the backbone. Then, she took the big bird by its feet and dipped it into the cauldron for a few seconds to scald it. When she removed it from the water, she lay it down on a nearby tree stump and began plucking the feathers. Once the feathers had all been removed, she opened the bird's body with a knife and removed its internal organs, saving the heart and liver. She handed the heart to David, and he promptly popped into his mouth and ate raw. She set aside the liver for later. She would add it to her gravy to put on top of her cornbread dressing. Lastly, she cut off the feet. She put the bird into an old flour sack and tied it up high out of reach of any critters that might come wandering through overnight. The temperature was quite cool outside, less than 40 degrees. It would probably reach freezing during the night, so there wasn't any worry of the meat becoming tainted. She would rise early the next morning and put him on a spit to roast on the fire for their Christmas meal at noon the next day. They all parted ways, beginning their various chores of the day. David went to the stables to tend to the horses. Sarah went inside to prepare lunch. Daniel found an axe and began splitting firewood.

December 25, 1817—Christmas Morning

Daniel awakened just as the sun began to peek inside his window. Jake seemed in no hurry to stir. He watched Daniel with only his eyes as Daniel rose and dressed. Sarah was already outside, starting a fire and setting up the spit to roast the turkey for their Christmas dinner. Sarah noticed him as he stepped out of his room. "There's some biscuits and bacon there on the table if you're hungry," she yelled to him.

"Thanks!" he yelled back.

He made a sandwich of bacon and biscuits and handed Jake a biscuit. He found a cup and poured himself a cup of coffee, then sat down in a chair to watch as Sarah prepared the turkey. The morning air was cold, and Daniel's light windbreaker did little to reflect that cold. He decided to move closer to the fire to feel its warmth. As he approached, he asked, "Need any help?"

"Yes. Can you help me lift the turkey up, so we can get him started cooking?"

Sarah had already run the spit through the bird, and Daniel helped her lift it into place onto the upright post. One of the posts had an eye hole on top of it. The spit was threaded through that eye. The other end of the spit rested on a U-shaped bracket at the top of the other post. The spit had a handle on one end, allowing them to turn the spit so the meat would cook on all sides. Daniel offered to be the official "spit-turner." What else did he have to do? He didn't have to crank the handle continuously. He just needed to turn the bird often enough so it didn't burn on one side. He was also in charge of keeping the fire up. Sarah went back inside to start preparing the rest of their meal.

Daniel had plenty of time to let his mind wander. He thought of his newfound friends. How quick they were to take him in as a member of the family. He thought of the Gordons and how Dolly quickly recognized that he didn't belong there. But mostly, he thought of Emily. He missed her so much. He missed her wry sense of humor. He missed her smile. He missed the smell of her hair after she had showered. But most of all, he missed her touch. How would he ever make it until June without her near him?

At about 1 o'clock that afternoon, Sarah decided the turkey was ready to eat. She and Daniel removed the bird from the fire and the spit. They put it on a large wooden platter and brought it to the table inside the dogtrot, where they would eat their meal. She spread out the rest of their bounty beside the turkey. She had made cornbread dressing with gravy she had prepared from the turkey liver and bacon drippings. There were fried apples and roasted potatoes. She made a peach cobbler from peaches she had canned over the summer for dessert. They all ate until they couldn't eat anymore. Even Jake benefitted from the meal as David tossed him the two leg bones after David had eaten most of the meat from them. Jake was in heaven.

As they sat back from the table to allow their food to digest a bit, Sarah asked Daniel, "How would you be celebrating Christmas if you were back home with your wife?"

Daniel paused momentarily, then said, "Well, Emily would probably be working today. She is a nurse and works in the hospital. Someone always had to be there, and since she and I don't have young children, she usually volunteers to work on Christmas so that the other nurses can spend the day with their families. So after work, she'd come home. I would have supper waiting for her. Nothing fancy like we all just ate. Then, we would open our presents that we had bought for each other."

"You buy gifts?" she asked.

"Most of the time," he replied. "Sometimes gifts are made. But most folks where I come from don't have the time or the knowledge to make gifts. So they go to a store and buy something."

"Everyone must be rich!" said Sarah.

"Well, not everyone," Daniel said. "People are working all the time, yet they accomplish very little. Life is much more complicated. People work for money to spend on things that they don't really need and can't really afford."

"Well, we give each other gifts here too," she said.

Sarah and David stepped inside their cabin and came back out, holding a few parcels wrapped in flour sacks. As they sat down, Sarah handed David one of the parcels. When he opened it, his eyes lit up with delight. Sarah had made him a new buckskin shirt. The shirt was decorated with designs she had added with dye she made from poke berries. David nodded in approval and said, "Thank you."

He then handed Sarah a small parcel, which she unwrapped. Inside was a very intricately carved wooden comb, which she could wear in her hair. "Oh, David! It's beautiful!" she exclaimed. "Thank you so much!"

Then she turned to Daniel and said, "We've got something for you, too." She handed Daniel one of the parcels, and David handed him another.

Daniel said, with surprise in his eyes, "Well, this is unexpected. Both of you shouldn't have gotten me anything." He opened the first parcel from

David, and inside was a furry ball of something that he hadn't recognized at first. As he moved it around in his hands, he realized it was a fur hat.

"Wow, this is great!" he exclaimed. "What kind of fur is this?"

Sarah replied, "It's beaver."

David pointed to the hat, then to his own head, and said, "Keep head dry. Keep head warm."

Daniel asked, "David, did you make this?"

David nodded his head slightly and replied, "Hmph!"

Before Daniel's delight had a chance to wear off, Sarah reminded him he had another parcel to open. Daniel opened the flour sack and pulled out the gift. His eyes widened as he saw what was inside. He pulled out a buckskin coat. It was heavy, and it would be warm, but it was also ornate. A short fringe dangled from the yoke of the garment, both front and back. The front could be fastened closed with wooden toggles looped through holes made from leather lace stitched onto the front of the jacket.

"This is amazing!" Daniel cried out. "Sarah, this is beautiful!"

"Try it on," she said.

Daniel tried on the coat, and the fit was just right. It was heavier and warmer than he thought it might be, but then he realized something.

"Sarah, you made this for David, didn't you?"

"I did," she replied. "But I talked to him about it, and we agreed that you needed a coat much more that he did. I told him I'd make him another one."

Daniel turned to David with tears in his eyes and said, "Thank you both so much!"

Then his eyes widened, and Daniel blurted out, "Oh, I have something for both of you as well."

He ducked into his room, then came back out holding his saddlebags. He reached into the bags and brought out his hunting knife. He handed it to David and said, "I want you to have this."

David took the knife from Daniel and pulled it out of its sheath. He saw how shiny the blade was and stared at it with delight. He turned it over in his hands and felt the sharpness of the blade against his thumb. David said, "Good knife. Thank you."

Daniel replied, "You are welcome, my friend."

Sarah was amazed, too, and asked, "What's it made of, Daniel? I've never seen a knife like that."

Daniel replied, "It's called stainless steel. I have no idea how it's made. I only know that as long as you keep it clean and dry, it will continue to shine like that."

Daniel reached back into the saddlebags and brought out his gift for Sarah.

"Here, Sarah. This is for you."

Sarah opened her mouth with amazement when Daniel handed her the Yeti thermos.

"What is it, Daniel?"

"It's called a thermos. It is also made of stainless steel, but it's a brushed stainless-steel finish."

Sarah stared at it and asked, "What do you do with it?"

Daniel took the thermos from her and said, "Here, you unscrew this top, and look, it's a cup. Then you take this little cap off and inside you can store hot coffee or soup or even something cold like fresh spring water. Whatever you put in will stay either hot or cold for as long as a couple of days. Now, you can fix yourself a thermos of coffee to take with you while you're working outside, and the coffee will keep you warm."

"Well, thank you, Daniel. Isn't that something?"

CHAPTER 8

T he next morning, Daniel awoke to the sun beaming through his window. It was cold outside. The temperature inside the cabin wasn't much warmer. The fire in his little stove was nearly burned out. Only a few embers still glowed inside the hopper. He added a few sticks of wood to the stove and stoked it to bring it back to life. A small flame slowly rose and began to burn the small sticks Daniel had added. He would be leaving soon, but he felt he should keep the fire going for whoever might need a room for the night.

He washed and dressed, donning his new buckskin coat and carrying his new fur hat. He grabbed his saddlebags and made sure he had packed everything back into them, then draped it over his right shoulder and walked out the door. Jake followed closely behind. When he walked out into the dogtrot, he saw Sarah and David sitting down to breakfast. He joined them at the table. Seeing Daniel carrying his saddlebags, Sarah asked, "Are you leaving today?"

"Yes. I want to get back to the Gordon place and talk to Dolly about the things I've learned from you and David. She might have an idea of what I should do about getting back when the time is right and what I should do in the meantime."

They all sat at the table, eating their breakfast in relative silence. The only noise they made was the occasional munching of their food. After a while, Daniel broke the silence and said, "You two just don't know how much it means to me for you to have taken me in these past few days. You've given me a lot to think about. I need to find more answers and I feel that I can't find those answers by hiding out in one place for the next six months. I need to move around and explore the area. Talk to more people. Learn as much as I can."

With sad eyes, Sarah replied, "We have enjoyed having you here. We hope you will come back, soon. Just remember, if things don't work out for you, you have family right here."

"I won't forget," he told her.

After breakfast, Daniel walked over to the corral and saddled Hoss. He threw his saddlebags over the back of his saddle and tied them on. He then led the horse up to the cabin to say his final goodbyes to his newly found family. When Sarah walked up to him, Daniel reached out his hand awkwardly, not knowing how to say goodbye to them. Sarah ignored the gesture and reached up and grabbed him around the neck to give him a bear hug. In return, he wrapped his free arm around her while holding onto the reins with his other hand. Once she had let go of him, he saw tears streaming down her cheeks. Daniel looked over at David and saw him nod in approval. Daniel shook David's hand and said, "Goodbye, my new friend."

David gave a slight smile and said, "See you soon."

Daniel mounted the big bay and turned him northeast toward the Duck River, and they headed down the Natchez Trail with Jake in tow.

~~~~~~~~~~~~~~~~~~~~

About an hour down the trail, Daniel noticed Hoss tense a little. Jake, too, had heard something in the distance. He gave a low growl, and the hair on his back bristled. Daniel pulled up to listen. A slight breeze was blowing from the north, bringing voices of men off in the distance. Daniel had no idea who it would be. He knew so few of the people in this area. However, he knew from his studies of the area that the Natchez Trail was notorious for scoundrels and thieves. Daniel thought it best not to take any chances with meeting someone on the trail. After all, he was unarmed and still out of his element. He dismounted his horse and quickly but silently led him southeast into the forest. He would need to move as far off the trail as possible so as not to be seen by whoever was approaching because the winter weather had stripped most of the trees of their foliage. Moving through the forest silently was nearly impossible as well. The fallen leaves crunched under their feet with every movement they made.

Daniel could only hope the sounds of the riders' own movements would hide the sounds of his. As Daniel led his horse, he walked closely to Hoss's head, cradling his muzzle to keep the horse from snorting or whinnying a warning to the riders' mounts. Daniel found a limestone outcropping about one hundred yards off the trail surrounded by cedars. He led Hoss and Jake behind the rocks and waited for the riders to pass. After ten minutes or so, Daniel saw the men moving up the trail, heading toward Sarah's stand. He watched them through the branches of two low-growing cedars. He counted four men, all well-mounted. They were dressed in frontier garb. Each man wore a brace of pistols draped over his shoulder, and he carried a long rifle in his free hand. If not looking for trouble, they were at least ready for it.

Daniel lay in wait for another five minutes once the party of riders left his sight. He couldn't get rid of a bad feeling he had in his gut about the men. Something just didn't feel right to him. He decided he would follow them back to Sarah's. Rather than walking back to the trail and following directly behind the riders, he chose to parallel the trail from his present distance and travel through the forest. It would take a little longer, but it would be safer for him in the end. He kept moving through the forest as quickly as possible, but he eventually had to return to the trail. He was far enough back now that he wouldn't be discovered. His adrenaline level was up. His senses were heightened. He could hear the riders in the distance faintly. As he got closer to the stand, he could smell the wood smoke from the fire burning in Sarah's cabin. When Daniel realized he was within spitting distance of the clearing where the cabin rested, he moved back into the brush and tied Hoss to a small dogwood tree. On foot, he and Jake circled through the forest to the eastern side of the clearing, on the back side of the cabin. There, he watched and waited. From here, Daniel could see the men more clearly. By 1800s standards, the men were pretty large in stature. The tallest was still only about 5'10"—much smaller than Daniel's 6'2". Three of the men were probably in their mid-twenties. The fourth was just a boy, maybe seventeen years old.

The ill intent of these men became evident very quickly. The boy and one of the men rode toward the corral where David was working. The other two stayed by the cabin and were speaking to Sarah. Daniel couldn't hear the conversation, but their mannerisms made it clear they were here to rob and maybe even kill the inhabitants of this domicile. Daniel could see right through the dogtrot, but his vision was obstructed whenever the men moved past the entrance.

"Jake, stay!" Daniel told the dog.

Jake whimpered but obeyed. Daniel moved back around to the front of the house, still concealing himself in the brush that surrounded the clearing. He could see the two men down at the corral were dismounting and approaching David now.

At the cabin one of the men had moved inside the cabin and was ransacking the place, looking for something. The other man held Sarah at bay. Suddenly, the man grabbed Sarah and held her in a bear hug. His back was to Daniel. Daniel looked around for anything to help him as a weapon. He saw it. The ax was still planted in the stump where he had been splitting firewood the day before. Daniel leaped from the brush, running toward Sarah's assailant. As he passed the stump, he grabbed the ax and lifted it above his head. He was running out of time, however, because the man had lifted his knife from his belt sheath and was bringing it above his body, ready to plunge it into Sarah. Daniel stopped suddenly, then flung the ax from his hands. The ax twirled through the air, end over end, until it landed squarely into the man's backbone. The man froze. His grip on Sarah was released, and she fell away from him. The ax must have severed his spine because he didn't die right away, but he couldn't move from where he fell on the ground. He screamed in pain, which alerted the man inside the cabin. The second man came running out with a pistol in hand. He moved toward Daniel, pointing the gun at him.

"Jake!" shouted Daniel.

Jake ran through the dogtrot and jumped at the man, biting his arm that brandished the pistol. A shot rang out as the gun expelled its load, but it missed its mark. Daniel continued running toward the man, reached out, and grabbed the spit rod that was still by the fire where they had roasted the Christmas turkey. He drove the spit into the man's chest like a knight on horseback thrusting his lance. Daniel and the man tumbled to the ground. When Daniel was able to get up, he saw that the spit had pierced the man's heart. His eyes were frozen, wide open. He gurgled on the blood that rose into his throat, and blood ran from the corners of his mouth. He coughed and spit as he choked on his own blood.

Daniel looked at Sarah and asked, "Are you all right?"

Trembling, she nodded but was unable to speak. Finally, she muttered, "David!"

Daniel looked back to the corral. David stood inside the corral, tending to the horses, when the boy and the third man rode up. His senses told him right away that they were trouble. The boy made the mistake of climbing over the corral gate on the opposite side of the pen, expecting to hem David up so his partner could ambush him from behind. David was holding onto the halter of a green-broke little colt when the kid approached. When the boy walked up behind the colt, making his way toward David, David yanked on the reins, which irritated the colt. Sensing something coming up behind him, the colt kicked hard with his right rear leg, sending his message into the crotch of the boy, who doubled over and rolled around in pain in a pile of horse manure.

The older man was already climbing over the fence, but he was too slow. David released the reins of the colt and reached for his brand-new knife. Before the man could swing one leg over the fence, David grabbed him by his shirt and jerked him to the ground. He took out his knife and plunged it into the man's throat, then sliced through his neck until his jugular was severed. Blood rushed from his throat as the Duck River flows. The cut took the man's head halfway off his body. David then moved to the boy. He grabbed the boy by his hair and slid his knife along the kid's throat, slicing him from ear to ear. Blood was everywhere. The boy's eyes stared in lifeless shock. David then cleaned his new knife on the boy's shirt. He grabbed the top rail of the fence and swung his body over it with his knife still in the other hand. He trotted up to the cabin to check on Sarah. There, he found Daniel standing over the other two men. One dead, the other still moaning in pain from his severed spine. David walked over to the dead man and checked him. Then, he moved over to the man who was moaning from his wounds. He took his knife and finished him. Four men all lay dead. David looked at Daniel and nodded in approval of how he had handled himself in protecting Sarah.

David walked over to Sarah and took his wife by the hand to raise her from the ground where she sat. He escorted her into their cabin, sat her down in her favorite chair, poured her a cup of coffee, and sat silently with her for a moment. Daniel walked back into the forest to retrieve his horse. He tied Hoss to a hitching rail just outside the cabin.

There were now four horses wandering around in the clearing of the stand, nibbling on the sparse brown grass scattered about. Daniel walked out carefully and captured them one by one. He deposited each one into the corral and unsaddled them. The saddles were placed on the ground outside the corral so he and David could examine them more closely later.

Daniel dragged each man from the corral and placed them near the forest's edge. It would be up to David to decide what they should do with the bodies. He then moved over to the cabin where the other two bodies lay. He untied Hoss from the rail and used him to pull the bodies over to the area where he had left the other two. He then led Hoss back to the corral, unsaddled him, and put him into the corral with the other horses.

David finally walked out of the cabin and met Daniel by the bodies.

"Any idea who they were?" Daniel asked.

"Never see before," David replied.

Daniel knelt down next to one of the bodies and began going through his pockets, searching for clues as to who the men might have been. He found a silver pocket watch without a chain, forty silver dollars, and some folded papers. He opened the papers and found a letter instructing the bearer that the target was M. Lewis. The letter wasn't signed, but the initials TJ were at the bottom of the letter. The top of the letter was dated September 3, 1809. Daniel folded the letter up and put it in his pocket. He stripped the man of anything that might be useful, taking his brace of pistols, powder horn, musket ball sack, and two knives. David started working on one of the other men. They stripped the men of everything except their clothes. They were too bloody and too full of holes to be of any use. Daniel looked at David and asked, "Where should we bury them?"

David pointed to the cabin and replied, "She boss!"

Daniel smiled a little smirk and nodded in agreement. They took their plunder, dropped it off with the saddles outside the corral, and then walked back to the cabin. By that time, Sarah had moved outside to the dogtrot, where she was sitting at the table. Daniel looked at her and asked, "Are you all right?"

She replied, "Much better, now."

"What do you want us to do with the bodies?" Daniel asked.

Sarah looked at him with hate in her eyes and responded, "They don't deserve a proper burial. Burn them! Burn them to hell!"

~~~~~~~~~~~~~~~~~~~~

That afternoon, Daniel and David worked, bringing logs and branches to the edge of the clearing for the fire they intended to build. They would gather pine, spruce, fir, and other softwoods full of sap. The sap would cause the fire to burn fast and hot, and these woods were unsuitable for use in the fireplace. Hardwoods were better for cooking and keeping the cabin warm. When they gathered enough wood, they built a platform to place the bodies. They lifted the bodies onto the platform and started a small brush fire underneath. As the fire gathered momentum, they added larger pieces of wood and piled them up so the flames would reach above the platform and consume the bodies. The fire eventually became so hot that David and Daniel could feel the warmth of its flames from the front of the cabin. The smell of burning hair and flesh was overwhelming. It took several hours for the bodies to be completely consumed. It was well into the night before the fire died down enough for the men to approach it. As they all retired for the night to their beds, they found sleep hard to come by, partly from concern that the fire might accidentally spread and ignite the forest but mostly from the thought of that day's events.

The next morning, as they sat down for breakfast, Sarah asked Daniel, "What made you come back, yesterday?"

"About an hour down the trail, Jake and Hoss heard the men coming. I thought it best that we get off the trail since I was unarmed and not knowing many folks from around here. I didn't know who I could trust. When I saw them heading up here, I decided to follow. They just didn't seem right to me."

Sarah said, "You have good instincts, Daniel. And because you were willing to act on those instincts, you saved my life. I can't thank you enough for that." Tears welled up in her eyes.

Daniel was glad Sarah was alive and well. He had killed a man and severely wounded another. He wasn't sure how he felt about that. He would absolutely do it again if faced with the same situation. He was beginning to realize that living in the early 1800s would not be like living in the twenty-first century. Law and order were scarce here. If he were going to survive, he would need to learn everything he could about survival.

After breakfast, Daniel and David walked to the corral. They still had not gone through the items they had scavenged from their attackers. David pointed to the plunder and said, "You keep half."

Daniel shrugged his shoulders and answered, "Alright."

The two of them went through the gear together, placing items as they came to them in one of two piles. They started with the larger items. There were four saddles and bridles. Four bedrolls. Four long rifles. Six pistols with four braces. Eight powder horns and four sacks filled with musket balls. Four water bags. Six hunting knives of various sizes. Two tomahawks. A set of cooking pans and utensils. Twelve more dollars in gold and silver coins. The silver watch without a chain. A silver comb and mirror with a handle. In the saddlebags of the man who Daniel killed were two leather-bound books. He opened them up to find that one was a ledger listing items that had been purchased. The other was a handwritten journal. He couldn't see who had written the journal at a quick glance. He set it aside and decided to look at it more carefully later. Daniel ended up with two of the horses, two saddles, two bedrolls, two rifles, three pistols, two of the braces, four powder horns, two sacks of musket balls, two water bags, two knives, one of the tomahawks, the cooking set and utensils, twenty-six dollars in coins, the watch, and the two books.

Then he asked David if he would teach Daniel how to load and shoot the rifles and pistols. David was happy to do so. The two of them spent the next two hours working on loading and firing the weapons. David also instructed him on how to keep the weapons cleaned and oiled. Daniel knew he had a good teacher. He had seen David make that shot on the turkey earlier in the week. The rest of the day was spent working around the stand.

David tended to the horses, checking and trimming their feet and brushing them down. Daniel spent a good part of the day splitting more firewood. It was mindless work that allowed him to think of other things. What would be his next move? What was Emily doing? Would they ever see each other again?

~~~~~~~~~~~~~~~~~~~~

Daniel ended up spending the winter with the Colberts. He no longer felt the urgent need to return to the Gordon place. He spent his time there, under David's tutelage. He learned about trapping, hunting, fishing, planting, and even fighting on the frontier. Most importantly, David taught Daniel the language of Chickasaw. David was pleased with his student's progress. Daniel learned quickly. He turned out to be the marksman with the rifle and pistol. His hand-to-hand combat skills became well-developed, and his ability to hit a target with the tomahawk was almost natural. And why not? He had already shown his ability to split a man's backbone with an ax from twenty paces.

When April came, Daniel decided it was time to move on. He still had places he wanted to explore, and he still needed to talk to Dolly Gordon about his situation. So, after saying his goodbyes to his new family, Daniel packed up his gear on the three horses he now owned, then headed back to the Duck River. This time, without incident. He, his three horses, and Jake were the only ones on the trail.

When they reached the river, Daniel saw the ferry was on the other side of the river. He noticed for the first time that a triangle bell hung on a post next to the ferry dock. He rang the bell to get Gus's attention. Gus turned and saw Daniel waving to him, and he waved back. It took Tom and Gus ten minutes to move the ferry over the river to meet Daniel. When Gus recognized that Daniel was the one calling for the ferry, he called out, "Well, Dan'l. How ye be?"

"Hi, Gus, Tom," he replied. "I'm doing well."

"Looks like you prospered a bit since we seen you last. Where'd you get them fine animals?"

Daniel explained, "David Colbert and I had a run-in with a band of bushwhackers a couple of months back. They left all their horses and gear with us for all the trouble they caused."

Gus responded, "Well, now ain't dat sumpin'? Let's git 'um all loaded up and git you cross, then."

Daniel led the animals onto the ferry, tied them all to the side rails, and prepared for the ten-minute journey back across the Duck. When they finished crossing, Daniel unloaded the horses along with Jake. He then asked Gus, "How much do I owe you?"

Gus responded, "Well, as far as I know, yer still a guest of Miss Dolly."

Daniel replied, "I appreciate that, but I can pay now. What's your usual fee?"

Gus thought while rubbing his beard and responded, "Well, we usually git two bits a man and two bits fer each of his horses, so I guess a dollar should cover it."

Daniel reached into his pocket and found his small leather pouch containing his money, then gave Gus two dollars.

"Here", he said. "Here's an extra dollar for you and Tom to split."

Gus' eyes lit up, and he tipped his hat and said, "Thank ya, Dan'l. That's mighty Christian of ye."

Daniel smiled and said, "I'll see you two tonight at supper." Then, he led his string of horses up the slope toward the Gordon camp.

When Daniel reached the camp, he saw that a lot of progress had been made on the Gordon House. They had finished laying brick on the outer walls. Brick walls on a house built in 1818 were rare in the frontier. Most likely, they were very common in Nashville, but all structures built along the Trace were built of logs. As he walked toward the house, Titus came through the open door of the structure and paused before turning back and speaking to someone inside the house. A moment later, Dolly came to the door. "Why, Mr. Lane. It's so good to see you again. How are you doing?"

"I'm doing very well," he said.

"Looks like you've added some horses since you left us," she said.

"Yes, ma'am. I'll tell you all about it this evening. That is if you'll allow me to stay a while."

Dolly said, "You're welcome to stay as long as you like. Of course, we might ask you to help out with some of the chores while you're here."

Daniel smiled and said, "It would be my pleasure to help in any way I can. I'll just put these horses in the corral and be right back."

Daniel led the horses into the corral, where they mingled and fed with the other horses. He then took his gear to the camp and lay it near one of the tables. When he got back to the house, he walked inside to find Dolly. She was supervising the men who were working inside the house. Titus was working with the men outside who were sawing boards. Daniel saw that shiplap was being nailed up on the interior walls when he walked in. He found a hammer lying on a sawhorse nearby and picked it up. He found the keg that contained the nails the men were using, grabbed a handful, and went to work nailing up the shiplap along with the other men. Dolly was pleased to see him jump right in to help. Daniel was by no means a carpenter, but he did know how to drive a nail. He had driven plenty of them while building their little barn back home. They all worked quickly yet skillfully, covering the house's interior walls. The evening light faded quickly, and Dolly announced soon it was time to quit.

They all left the work area and went outside to wash for supper. The slave women had everything prepared for the evening meal as they approached the camp dining area. The Gordon clan came in from all parts of the farm to gather for the evening meal. They all took their usual places, and Dolly motioned for Daniel to take a seat next to her as she sat at the head of one of the tables. Everyone sat and waited for Dolly's instructions. "Micah, I believe it is your turn to say grace."

Micah, who was now sixteen, recited the prayer that he had been taught, no doubt, at a very early age. "Bless us, O Lord, and these Thy gifts which we have received from Thy bountiful hand. Amen!"

As the meal progressed, Dolly asked Daniel about his time away from them, how he came to have two extra horses and weapons, and everything else he now carried. Daniel described in great detail his adventures while staying at Sheboss Stand. He, however, left out some of the gruesome details of the men that he and David had killed. After they finished eating, Dolly asked, "Mr. Lane, will you walk with me, please?"

The two of them walked away from the others to have a private conversation. "Did you find the answers you were looking for?" she asked.

Daniel responded, "Yes, I think so. David was able to provide me with information about how I might have come here. May I ask, how did you know?"

Dolly answered, "I didn't know. At least I wasn't sure. I just suspected."

Daniel asked, "So you know about Ittola Chuka?"

"Ittlola Chuka?" she asked. "No, I've never heard of it. What is it?"

Daniel explained, "Ittola Chuka is the Chickasaw word for 'Shimmering Door.' It is the gateway that brought me here from my time."

"What year did you come here from?" she asked.

"Twenty-seventeen," he answered. "Two-hundred years from when we are right now."

"Did David know of a way for you to return?" she asked.

Daniel thought before he answered. "*Why wasn't she more shocked about the amount of time that he had traveled to be here*?" he thought. Then he said to her, "Ittola Chuka evidently opens up twice a year during the winter solstice and the summer solstice. The only way for me to get back is to go back the way I came. It would be dangerous, though. Ilbuk Losa are watching that area whenever it occurs."

"Ilbuk Losa?" she asked.

"The Black Hand," he translated.

"Do you plan to try?" she asked.

"I have to," he answered. "It's the only way I'll ever see my wife again."

"When the time comes, I'll do whatever I can to help you get back to her. In the meantime, you're welcome to stay here as long as you like."

Daniel said, "I appreciate your help and your offer. I would like to set up my base camp here if you don't mind. But I want to do some exploring while I'm here. I studied history at college, and I'm particularly fond of the history of this area. I know Meriwether Lewis died about two days ride from here at Grinder's Stand. I'd like to ride over there and do some poking around."

Daniel didn't tell Dolly about the two books he had pillaged from the man he had killed. He had discovered that the books belonged to Meriwether Lewis. They evidently were stolen at the time of his death by whoever had killed him.

With a concerned look, Dolly replied, "You just be careful around here. Folks aren't as civilized around here as what you're probably used to."

"I will. And thanks for everything."

Dolly walked back toward the group of people still hovering around the eating area of the camp. As she passed by Gus she touched him on the shoulder and asked, "Are you going to tell him?"

Gus looked up at her sheepishly and nodded. Tom looked at him, then looked at her and asked, "What did she mean, Gus? Who's she talking about?"

"Never mind," said Gus. "You stay here. I got sumppin' to do."

Gus walked away from the table and moved to where Daniel was still standing. Daniel had his back to Gus as he approached. When he drew near, he cleared his throat and said, "Uh, Daniel?"

Daniel turned to see who it was and replied, "Hey, Gus. How... what did you call me?"

"Daniel," Gus replied.

"What happened to your accent?" asked Daniel.

"Oh, well that's kind of what I wanted to talk to you about," said Gus. "That accent is all for show. It helps me fit in a little better. Makes people less suspicious of me. Especially when I first got here."

"Got here?" asked Daniel. "Where did you come from?"

Gus's sheepish look returned to his face once again as he answered, "Nineteen seventy-three."

Daniel's eyes widened in shock.

Gus reached into the shoulder bag draped across his body and pulled out a piece of colorful cloth. He handed it to Daniel for him to inspect. "I was wearing this when I came through."

Daniel unfolded the cloth and discovered it to be a tie-dyed T-shirt. Daniel tried to do the math in his head. "So you've been here, what, forty-five years?"

"Yep," replied Gus. "My name is August Moon Earthchild. I lived with my family in Summertown. My folks moved to Summertown from California to start a commune. I was raised there. We were big into natural remedies and herbal medicines and such, so my friend, Robbie Sunflower, and I were sent to find some of the herbs we needed. We came down the Natchez Trace in our VW bus and stopped in this area to begin our search. We spent half a day looking around for sage, lavender, peppermint, whatever we could find. We ended up in this open field back that way."

He pointed toward the way that Daniel had come in originally. "We got separated from each other. I found a bunch of blackberries that I started gathering while Robbie was in that open field. I heard him scream. When I looked around, I saw Indians riding away from him. They had killed him. Evidently, they hadn't seen me. I waited until I was sure they were gone before I moved out of the briars where I was picking the berries. By then, it was dark. I tried to pick up Robbie and carry him back to the bus, but he was too heavy for me. So I decided to go and find help. I wandered around all night, trying to find my way back to the bus. I never did find it. When the sun rose, I finally figured out that I wasn't in the same place I had been the day before. Robbie's body was still there, but the landscape was different. There wasn't a bus to go back to. I was scared. Too scared to venture out very far. I stayed in the area for what seemed like years before I saw anyone that wasn't Indian. After a time, a white man showed up. His name was Timothy Demonbreun; he was a trapper from Illinois and he taught me how to trap and survive out here alone. Later on, more men and women showed up and built a fort. That's where I eventually met the Gordons. Then, about five years ago, Captain Gordon and his wife started the ferry and hired me to run it for him. Mrs. Gordon is the only one that knows about me."

Daniel started working things out in his head. "David Colbert told me that a man passed through the Ittola Chuka many years ago. His elders used to tell stories about the man. But he said the man was killed as soon as he passed through. He was the only one to pass through until I did last December."

Gus replied, "They must be thinking of Robbie. I didn't let any of them see me. They didn't know I passed through." Gus continued, "Daniel, did you find a way back through?"

Daniel nodded his head, "I think so. David said that the gateway opens twice a year, during the winter and summer solstice. If we can find the exact spot where the gateway opens and be there when it opens, we should be able to get back to my time at least."

Gus thought for a second, then asked. "When is your time?"

Daniel replied, "It was 2017 when I came through."

CHAPTER 9

Friday, April 6, 2018: Emily slept in for a change. It was the first day of her vacation. She wouldn't be returning to work until April sixteenth. She had a lot to accomplish in the next ten days, but that didn't mean she couldn't allow herself a little extra sleep. Besides, most Columbia businesses wouldn't be open until 10:00 a.m. anyway. She had planned two things for today's agenda. She had scheduled a meeting with her lawyer, Robert Samuels, at 3:00 p.m.; secondly, she planned to talk to a man about a pair of mules. Today was the first full day of the Mule Day Celebration in Columbia. She normally despised Mule Day because of the traffic it brought to the small community. The celebration usually brought in an extra fifty thousand to as many as one hundred thousand people into the community. Since most of them were riding on horses, mules, or wagons, traffic was usually held at a snail's pace. However, she saw this year's celebration as an opportunity to buy the pair of mules she would need for her journey to meet Daniel, as well as a wagon. She wouldn't be buying today, just making contacts for when the time was right. Mule breeders from all over the southeast would be at the event, and she needed to find the right breeder to get exactly what she needed.

She had called Tommy Brown, the park ranger who had helped her search for Daniel, to come over and help her with her search. She also planned to spring her plans on Tommy in hopes he would be willing to help her. Tommy was scheduled to arrive at 9:00 a.m., so when she rose at 7 o'clock, she had given herself just two hours to look after the animals, bathe, and cook breakfast for the two of them. She quickly got dressed and walked up to the barn. She didn't bother with milking. She only gathered the eggs, let the goats out of their pens to graze, and she fed the mare who now had a new beautiful little colt. It only took her fifteen minutes to handle everything at the barn, then she was back at the house and into the shower.

By 8:00 o'clock, she was making scratch biscuits, frying bacon, and scrambling eggs for her breakfast with Tommy. The eggs were coming out of the skillet at nine o'clock, just as Tommy rang the doorbell. When Emily opened the front door, she greeted him with a huge smile and said, "Come on in, Tommy. Thanks for coming over today."

Tommy replied, "Anything for you, Emly."

She escorted him to the dining table and had him sit across from her. They spent the next few minutes eating their breakfast and making small talk about the weather, how Tommy was getting along, how Ranger Douglas was, and whatever else came to mind. Once they had finished their meal, Emily took the opportunity to present her plans to Tommy.

"Tommy," she began, "I now know what happened to my husband out on the Trace. At least in part, that is."

Tommy raised his eyebrows questioningly and asked, "Well, what happened to him?"

Emily got up from the table and went into her bedroom to retrieve the chest her grandfather had given her. She brought it back and lay it on the table in front of Tommy.

Then she began, "The chest has proof of what I'm about to tell you. It was given to me by my grandfather on the day that you and I met. The day after Daniel and Jimmy disappeared. Do you remember when you and I followed their tracks, how they just seemed to vanish?"

"Yes," Tommy responded.

"Do you remember the date?"

Tommy thought for a moment. "No, I don't rightly know."

Emily continued, "They disappeared on December twenty-first. That is the winter solstice, the shortest day of the year."

Tommy said, "Okay, that sounds about right."

Emily cautiously began, "You're going to find this hard to believe, but on the day of the solstice, there evidently is an occurrence which happens at that spot where Daniel's tracks ended. A sort of gateway opens up between two different time periods. Jimmy and Daniel went back in time by passing through that gateway."

Tommy looked at her with astonishment and asked, "How do you know this?"

Emily opened up the small chest in front of Tommy and said, "It's all right here."

First, she removed Davy Crockett's letter and carefully handed it to Tommy. "Read this," she said.

Tommy carefully took the letter from her and read it silently moving his lips. Once he had finished, he started to lower the paper toward the table, but Emily said, "Wait, there's more."

She turned the paper over for him and showed him the timeline.

"These names listed on the back of this parchment paper are all descendants of Davy Crockett. This last one? That's my grandfather."

Tommy looked up at her and replied, "Wow, so you're a direct descendant of Davy Crockett?"

Emily nodded.

"But what's this got to do with time travel?" he asked.

Emily pulled out the second piece of parchment and handed it to him. "This was sealed in wax with my personal seal, the day my grandfather gave it to me. I broke the seal when I read it for the first time. As you can see, it is as old as the other parchment you just read."

Tommy examined the seal and then opened up the document and began to read. When he had finished reading, he looked up at her again and asked, "So you wrote this to yerself?"

Emily nodded again.

"And Davy Crockett kept this letter for you, passing it down to his kinfolk?"

Emily smiled at him and said, "You got it!"

"But how did you give this letter to Davy Crockett?" Tommy asked.

Emily chuckled as she said, "I don't really know. I guess I meet him sometime in the future, or not the future. I guess its the past. I have to get back to the 1800s to be with Daniel again."

Tommy asked, "Well, how ya gonna do that?"

"I've got to go through the gateway during the next solstice," she replied.

"Emly, you ain't foolin' with me are ya?"

"No, Tommy. This is all true. I promise!" Tommy thought for a moment, then said, "Well, what are you tellin' me all this fer?" Emily displayed a sinister smile on her face and said, "Because I need your help."

Emily laid out her plan for Tommy, leaving out a few of the details that he would discover later. By the time they had finished their discussion, it was 11:30 a.m. Emily asked, "What do you know about mules?"

"Well, I'm no expert. But my daddy had a couple of mules when I was growing up. Why?"

Emily answered with a question. "Can you go with me to Maury County Park? I want to buy a pair of mules."

~~~~~~~~~~~~~~~~~~~~

Emily and Tommy arrived at the park around noon. They each drove their own vehicles because Emily needed to meet her lawyer at 3:00 pm. There were a lot of people at the park, although not nearly as many as would be there the next day. Saturday was the main event for Mule Days. The parade in downtown Columbia would draw thousands of spectators. Most of the people present today were either food and craft vendors selling their wares or mule owners participating in the day's events, such as the mule pull. Emily and Tommy met at the arena where the pulling events would take place. Many of the people who came to Mule Day with their animals were there for nostalgic purposes. It was a time for them to ride around town on horseback or mule. Many of them rode in wagons pulled by either a pair of horses or mules. Some groups would arrive on Thursday by way of a caravan from as far away as Alabama. Very few of them were serious mule breeders. The ones who were, participated in the mule pulling events.

Emily and Tommy stood at the railing of the arena fence, watching the mules as they pulled their heavy loads. The teams were pulling across the arena while being timed. There were teams of mules about the size of an average saddle horse as well as mules that towered over their drivers. The draft mules were what Emily was most impressed with. They were nearly as large as a Clydesdale horse.

Emily and Tommy watched for about thirty minutes until the event came to a close. As the event coordinators began setting up the next event, Emily said to Tommy, "Come on."

She led him through the crowd back to the area where the mule exhibitors were camping. She followed a man with a long white beard who was leading a team away from the arena. Emily said, "When we get there, follow my lead." Tommy nodded.

The man reached his destination, tying the mules to the side of a stock trailer by their lead reins. Emily walked up behind the man and said, "Excuse me. You've got some really impressive animals there."

The man turned around to see who was talking. He was an older man who stood about six feet tall, though a little hunched back from years of being kicked, stepped on, and generally abused by his four-legged giants. When he saw a very attractive young woman complimenting his mules, he was pleased and gave her a grin.

"Well, thank you, young lady."

Emily reached out her hand to shake his and said, "I'm Emily Lane, and this is Ranger Tommy Brown."

"Ranger?" the man questioned.

"I'm with the National Park Service," he replied.

The old man greeted them both with a handshake and said, "Well, I'm pleased to meet you both. I'm Wesley Taylor."

"Mr. Taylor—" Emily began.

"Just Wesley, ma'am. You can call me Wes if you like."

"Thank you, Wes. I've been commissioned by the Park Service to set up an authentic display on the Natchez Trace. We're setting up a small area near the Gordon House to show what things looked like during the early 1800s. Tommy here is helping me to coordinate the display."

Wes responded. "Well, that sounds real interesting, ma'am. How can I help?"

"We need a working pair of mules for our exhibit. They need to be able to actually work a nineteenth-century farm. Pull a plow or wagon, as well as turn a grist wheel or sugar press. Do you have any mules you'd be willing to sell for this exhibit?"

Wes stood staring at the two of them for a moment, glancing back and forth between the two of them while Tommy stood by, nervously smiling and nodding his head in agreement with Emily.

Wes finally cracked a smile and responded, "Well, yeah, I've got lots of mules for sale. Shoot, these two here are my best team of pullers. I'll sell them for the right price."

Emily asked, "And what would be the right price?"

"Well, ma'am, a feller offered me $15,000 just yesterday for this pair. But I told him I wouldn't take less than $25,000."

Emily tried very hard not to let Wes see the shock in her eyes that she was feeling throughout her whole body. She responded after a moment by saying, "Hmm, that's a little out of our price range. We've only been budgeted $500,000 for the whole exhibit, buildings and all. I was thinking somewhere more in the range of $10,000 for the pair."

Wes responded, "Well I can't let these go at that price, but I've got lots of mule teams that would be in that price range. If you'd like to come out to my place sometime, I'd be more than happy to show you around."

Emily replied, "That sounds good. Where is your ranch?"

"Oh, it ain't a ranch, ma'am. Just a farm. Ranches is for uppity folks that's got too much money. I'm a working man. My farm is up on the Pulaski Highway, just inside the Giles County line. Here's my card. It's got my phone number and my address on it."

Emily took the card from his hand and asked, "Will you be available Monday?"

"I'll be there all day. Just give me a call to let me know what time to expect you, and I'll be there with bells on."

As Emily and Tommy walked away, Tommy asked Emily, "What did you need me for?"

Emily replied, "Sorry, Tommy, I needed you to give credence to my lies. I can't tell people what I'm really up to. If you're not comfortable with this, I'll understand."

Tommy said, "Naw, I found it kinda fun watching you spin all those yarns to him like that. I rather enjoyed it after I figured out what you was doing."

Emily smiled at him as they walked back to their cars. When they reached the cars, she turned to him and asked, "How much do you know about loading and shooting old guns?"

Tommy asked, "You mean like muzzleloaders?"

Emily nodded in reply.

"Well, I don't own any, but I used to shoot them a little when I was a boy with my daddy."

"Can you teach me?" Emily asked.

"Sure!" Tommy said. "But I don't have any to teach you with."

Emily smiled again and replied, "That's okay, I own a few. And I've got the ammo too."

Tommy raised his eyebrows in response and said, "You sure are full of surprises. Just give me a call when you get ready and I'll take you to the gun range to show you how."

Emily reached up and gave him a slight hug and said, "Thanks, Tommy, for everything." Then she got into her car and drove away.

Emily drove to the downtown area of Columbia to the office of Robert Samuels, attorney at law. His office was just off the square, where the Maury County courthouse was located. The downtown district was going through some major overhauls. Local businessmen were taking great strides in bringing back the old buildings that had stood empty and unused for decades. It was once an area in the small city that people and businesses avoided but now were scrambling for, trying to claim their spot. Parking could be a problem. Sometimes one might have to circle the square several times to find an available parking space. Although the parking was free, there was a two-hour limit, which was watched closely by a local parking monitor person. That didn't worry Emily. She didn't plan to be here more than an hour.

After two trips around the square, she pulled into a vacant spot just as another motorist was leaving. It was half a block away from the lawyer's office, and three o'clock was quickly approaching. She hurried around the corner and entered the building just as the big clock inside the courthouse chimed three times. As she walked in, she was greeted by an older lady who was sitting behind a desk. She was attractive and very stylish for a woman her age. When she spoke, it was evident to Emily that the woman's vocal chords had been attacked by many years of smoking. Her voice was deep and gravelly.

"May I help you?"

"I'm Emily Lane. I have a three o'clock appointment with Robert."

Without responding, the woman picked up the receiver of her phone and punched a button. "Mrs. Lane is here."

After a very brief moment, she responded to Emily, "He'll be right out."

Thirty seconds later, a tall thin man walked into the reception area through a doorway without a door. He was wearing a light-blue seersucker suit. Emily hadn't seen anyone wearing seersucker in years, and that was on an old TV show. Maybe it's coming back, she thought.

The man smiled and reached out to shake her hand. "Mrs. Lane?"

"Yes," she said. "Please call me Emily."

"All right. Come on back to my office."

He led her through a short hallway, which led to an office in the back. They passed two rooms along the way. A small room that was used as a break room, and then a bathroom.

"Come on in and have a seat," he said.

The office was not huge, but comfortable and well decorated. There were two large leather wingback chairs sitting in front of a huge mahogany desk. A built-in bookcase filled with law books lined the wall behind the desk.

As Emily sat down in one of the chairs he asked, "What can I do for you?"

Emily began, "My husband has been missing since December. He and a friend went on a trail ride on the Natchez Trace together and never came home. I met with the Park Rangers the day after, and we followed their trail until it came to an abrupt end. The police don't know what happened to him and the case has gone cold. I need to find him, but I want to set my affairs in order before I begin my search."

Samuels asked, "Do you have reason to believe you won't be coming back?"

Emily replied, "I don't know. I'm sure my husband had no reason to believe he wouldn't be coming back from his trail ride. But he didn't."

Samuels asked, "Do you have family you want to list as benefactors?"

"I do have family. My grandfather and my aunt. But they won't be listed. My grandfather is near the end of his life, and my aunt and I were never close. My husband doesn't have any family. His parents were killed in a car accident six years ago, and he was an only child."

"Then who will you list as a benefactor?" Samuels asked.

"I have someone in mind who has helped me tremendously through this ordeal," Emily replied.

The two continued to discuss the details of Emily's last will and testament, and Emily left the office. The meeting took a little longer than she had anticipated, but she still made it back to her car before the two-hour time limit. When she got into her car and started it, she didn't back out immediately. She pulled out her cell phone and called Hank Slater. A voice came on the phone and said, "Hello?"

"Hank, it's Emily Lane."

"Hi, Emily! How are you?"

She replied, "I'm fine. Look, I need to get the rest of my belongings from you. When can we meet?" Hank said, "Well, the park closes at 6 pm. Can you get here in the next fifteen minutes?"

"No, I'm in Columbia. How about tomorrow?"

Hank was silent for a moment then said, "The park opens at 7 a.m. I can meet you anytime after that."

Emily replied, "I'll see you at the museum at 7:15."

She hung up the phone, then backed out of her parking space and headed home.

When she got home, she quickly checked on the animals. She only did the basics; Food and water to sustain them. She didn't take time to milk her goat anymore. She let the kids nurse full-time now. She gathered eggs from the coop, but that was pretty much the extent of her animal husbandry these days. She knew as long as they all had access to food, water, and shelter, they would be fine.

When she got back to the house, she grabbed a TV dinner from the freezer and popped it into the microwave. That and a bottle of water would be enough for tonight. She was anxious to get back into her reading.

She had been doing a lot of reading lately. She read about natural healing techniques and herbal remedies. She read about the history of medicine and surgical techniques. She knew that if she was going to meet Daniel in the 1800s, she would need to be prepared. She would read articles online about the era. She had never been interested in history. Science was what she liked while growing up. But she went through Daniel's history books, looking for subject matter that related to her search. Tonight, while searching through his bookcase, she found his pride and joy. "A History of the People Who Lived Along the Natchez Trail" by Daniel Lane. Emily took the book from the shelf. She carefully held it in her hands as if she were holding a newborn baby. She realized she had not seen this book in a very long time. She had never read it. She had barely noticed it on Daniel's shelves. It had just been another of Daniel's old dusty books that she cared nothing about. But she felt the book calling to her now. She walked into the living room and sat down in her favorite chair. She took a deep breath and slowly opened the book with her trembling hands. Suddenly, all those lonely feelings she had felt after Daniel's disappearance came rushing back. The doubts of ever seeing him again began crushing her spirit once again. On the title page, she read,

"A History of the People Who Lived Along the Natchez Trail by Daniel Lane.

Originally Published 1840. Re-published 1980 by the National Park Service."

She turned to the next page where she read,

The Natchez Trail was established by the Federal government. An agreement was established between the government and local Indian tribes so that the trail could be used by travelers, soldiers, and freight companies who needed to reach the Gulf Coast. It was also used by Europeans and Settlers in the late 1700's and early 1800's to move from the Cumberland River area of Tennessee to the Mississippi River in Natchez, Mississippi. Although traders would use the trail, it was also frequented by bandits.

Settlers who lived along the trail in the early 1800's did so only by gaining permission from the Chickasaw nation and their leader, Chief William Colbert. They were allowed to set up trading posts and inns called stands. These stands were typically set up a day's ride from each other, providing safe havens for travelers along the trail. The people who were allowed to settle along the trail were hard-working people living simpler lives but living them to the fullest.

Emily gasped when she read that line. They were the words Daniel had spoken to her many, many times before. "We're gonna live simpler lives and live them to the fullest!"

Emily closed the book and began to weep uncontrollably.

Chapter 10

Saturday, April 7, 2018: Emily rose early to get ready for her meeting with Hank Slater. Because of the construction at the Highway 43 and Highway 166 intersection, she would have to detour to reach Lawrenceburg. She took the pickup truck to retrieve all her belongings from the museum. She grabbed a food bar and made herself an extra-large coffee to take with her as she headed out the door. She left the house at 6 o'clock. That would give her a fifteen-minute window if she runs into unexpected traffic. The drive was uneventful except for the two-state patrol vehicles she saw parked in the median at two different points of her journey. She was expecting them, however, and was vigilant in driving at the proper speed all along the way.

She reached the front gate of the park at 7 o'clock, just as rangers were opening the gates. There was one vehicle in front of her as she pulled through. She recognized it as Hank's. She followed him the entire way through the park until they reached the museum's parking lot. After they both parked, they got out and greeted each other as they made their way to the museum's front door. Hank noticed the small chest Emily was carrying but said nothing about it. As they made their way to the vault, Hank said, "I've left everything unpacked for you. I want you to verify that it is all there as we found it on your last visit. Then we can pack it all up and seal it with security tape. I've got four men who work on the grounds crew, coming in to help load everything. They should be here about 8 o'clock."

Emily replied, "That sounds good. Before they get here, I've decided to share some information with you."

Hank looked at the chest and asked, "Is that the chest Wild Bill gave you?"

Emily said, "It is."

She set it on top of one of the crates and opened it up. Then she removed the first parchment and handed it to Hank. He first noticed the writing on the outer side of the folded parchment. He read the lineage listing the names of Davy Crockett and his descendants to Emily's grandfather. He then opened up the parchment and looked it over intently. The first thing he noticed was the signature.

"The signature is authentic. I've seen it many times in my life. I have no doubt that this document is authentic."

He then read the document, and he first said, "This letter was written to his eldest son, two days before his death. This is quite a discovery!"

Emily then took the other parchment out of the chest and handed it to him. He set the first parchment down next to the opened chest and took the second from Emily's hand. He examined it, noting that it was enclosed in an envelope sealed with a wax seal and imprint. The imprint on the seal was the letters ECL. He opened the envelope and removed the enclosed parchment.

Emily asked, "How old do you think the parchment is?"

Hank responded, "I'd say that it is the same age as the other document. It has the same aging and yellowing that this first has. It feels the same, both are very delicate and frail."

Emily said, "Go ahead and read it, then."

Hank read it slowly to himself, lingering on every word. When he finished, he read it all again.

"I don't understand," he said. "Do you mean that you wrote this letter to yourself?"

"I did," she replied. "Hank, you've got to promise me that you won't tell anyone about this. No one can know!"

Hank said with an amazed look, "I promise I won't tell a soul."

"All right," she said. "Let's get these things crated back up and sealed before your guys show up."

They worked together, putting all the items back into their crates and nailing them shut. Then, they took some red security tape and applied it to each of the crates to seal them. If any of the seals were broken when she reached her destination, she would know someone had tampered with them. However, that would be very unlikely because she intended to drive straight home.

Hank's men showed up just as they sealed the last crate. Hank instructed them to carry the crates to the parking lot and load them into Emily's truck. There were eight crates in all. The four men only took fifteen minutes to carry them out and load them into the truck. Emily walked out with Hank once the last crate was removed from the vault. She carried her little chest with its contents as she walked. As they walked, Hank asked her, "Emily, you wouldn't consider leaving the documents with me for further inspection would you?"

"No, Hank," she replied. "These documents won't be leaving my sight."

Then he asked, "Uh, how about the other chest? The one you took with you last time you were here. Did you ever get it opened?"

She looked at him uneasily and replied. "Oh, yeah. It was just some old junk. Some letters and stuff. Nothing worth much."

Once they reached the cars, Emily climbed into the back of the truck, checked all the crates, and counted them to ensure they were all there. Satisfied that they were all accounted for, she jumped down and said goodbye to Hank, then got into the truck and drove away. As he watched her drive away, Hank pulled his cell phone out of his pants pocket and opened it up to his photos. He checked to see if he had gotten it. There it was. He had taken a photo of her letter while her back was turned. He allowed himself a wry little smile before he got into his car to drive away.

As Emily made the hour-long drive back home, she began to feel uneasy about showing Hank the documents. She started second-guessing herself. *Grandpa trusted Hank; why shouldn't I?* she thought to herself. Still, something told her deep inside that she should have listened to her own words from the letter: *Don't tell anyone except Grandpa and Tommy Brown. Don't trust anyone.* She decided she would take measures when she got home to ensure the safety of her secret.

When she got home, she left the crates in the back of the truck and parked it in the garage. She carried the small chest into the house and walked to the living room. On the hearth of the fireplace sat the larger chest containing all the gold and silver coins. If someone found the empty chest, they might be determined to look elsewhere for its missing contents. She decided to put something back into the chest and lock it back so no one could open it without considerable effort. She spotted just what she needed next to the front door. A large piece of limestone that she sometimes used as a doorstop. It had been left behind by the stonemasons who built their fireplace. It would fit inside the chest, and it weighed about twenty pounds. She retrieved the rock and placed it into the chest.

Just as she was about to close the chest, she decided to leave a message for any would-be thief. She found a large black magic marker and wrote a message onto the stone, then closed it and locked it. Then, she took the letters from the smaller chest and placed the one from Davy Crockett on the grate inside the fireplace. She grabbed a small butane lighter from the mantel and ignited the parchment. She watched it as it emitted a glowing light. In less than a minute, it was completely consumed. She folded the other letter and put it back into the envelope and then back into the chest.

Monday, April 9, 2018

Emily arrived at Wesley Taylor's mule farm at 1:15 p.m. It was a cloudy day, and a slight mist was falling, making it unusually cool for April. Wes met Emily as she exited her car and welcomed her with a hardy handshake. "How are ya, Miss Emily?"

"I'm fine, thank you," she replied. "So have you got some mules hanging around here you'd like to show me?"

Wes said, "Why shore! I got one or two hangin' around here and about."

They walked side by side as he gave her a tour of his place. He showed her the pastures that held most of his breeding stock. Then he showed her four large pens where most of the training was done. The pens were huge compared to the pens on her little farm. Each one was the size of a high school football field. Then he directed her to the barn. It was more like a five-star hotel for equine. There were forty stalls inside as well as hay storage upstairs and a large tack room at the end of the barn. It reminded her of some of the Tennessee Walking Horse barns she had seen in Bedford County. The mule business was almost as lucrative as the Walking Horse business.

As they walked through the barn, Wes described all the residents of the equine hotel, naming them off one by one. Emily noticed that some of the stalls were empty as they walked past them. When they reached the barn's end, Wes said, "I've had some of the boys pull out a few teams for you to get a closer look at. They're right back here in this small pen."

As they walked into the pen, she observed four pairs of mules tied to the fence rails on each side of the pen. The first pair were black.

"This here is Jack and Jill," Wes said. "They're both about twelve hands. Good-natured for mules and stout."

As they continued to walk, they came to the next pair, which were white with brown spots that reminded Emily of an Appaloosa horse. Wes announced, "This is Comanche and Pocahontas. They were both born out of Appaloosa mares. They're also about twelve hands high. Not quite as easy to get along with as the last two, but really strong."

The third pair they came to were brown with black manes and tails.

"Now Emily, I'm gonna test you a little to see what kind of horse person you might be. Can you tell me what color these two mules are?"

Emily said, "They're bays. That's easy. We have two bay horses on our farm. Well, actually, it's three now. Our mare just had a colt."

Wes smiled and said, "Well, congratulations! Now, these two are Levi and Lois. They're fifteen hands and very strong. They work real good together, and they have gentle dispositions."

Finally, they came to the last pair. An impressive pair of sorrels. Red bodies with blond manes and tails. These mules were enormous, although not nearly as big as the two mules she had seen with Wes at the park a few days earlier.

"Now these two are Rusty and Pepper. They are a whopping nineteen hands high. They look intimidating, but they *are* gentle. They work well together and they're *real* smart. Dollar for dollar, this is your best buy."

Emily walked to the animals, rubbed them on the face and muzzle, and spoke gently to them. They were beautiful animals, and Emily immediately fell in love with them.

"How much?" she asked.

"Twelve thousand for the pair," Wes replied.

Emily asked, "Does that include delivery?"

Wes said, "I'll deliver them up to two hundred miles for that price."

"How about harness?" she asked.

"I'll throw in the harness for free," Wes replied.

"Deal!" said Emily, holding out her hand to seal the deal. Then she asked, "Half now, half on delivery?"

Wes grabbed her hand and said, "Yes, ma'am, you gotta deal. Just give me your address, and I'll have them there on Saturday morning."

Emily asked, "Can I write you a check for the down payment? It will clear before Saturday if you deposit it tomorrow. Then I'll have cash for you on Saturday when you make the delivery."

Wes responded, "That'll be fine. Do you want me to make the bill of sale out to the Parks Service?"

Emily answered, "No, I'm going to loan them to the Park Service. But they will be mine. Make the bill of sale to Emily Lane."

"All right," he said. "I'll have that ready for you on Saturday then."

As Wes escorted Emily back to her car, she asked, "By the way, do you know anyone who builds authentic wagons?"

Wes replied, "I sure do. There's a feller over in Hohenwald who builds them. He builds all kinds. His name is Thomas Dellinger and he lives out on Highway 20 near the Trace."

"That's perfect!" she said. Then, the two of them said goodbye, and Emily drove away.

Emily was a little nervous on her drive back home. She had never made such a large purchase without Daniel being present. They had the money. Both she and Daniel had received inheritances when their parents died. Daniel got $100,000, and she got $50,000 from life insurance policies. They used most of it to pay off their mortgage, but about $55,000 was in their bank account. Emily had made the decision that the money would be spent on supplying her trip through time. She wouldn't be able to take the cash with her. It wouldn't be any good in 1818. On the other hand, the gold and silver in her freezer would be going with her.

When Emily reached her house, she decided to call Thomas Dellinger to make an appointment to meet with him. She reached him and made the appointment for the next day at 10 a.m. She spent the rest of her day shopping online for essential oils, medical supplies, and heritage garden seeds.

Tuesday, April 10, 2018

Emily pulled into Thomas Dellinger's driveway at five minutes until ten. Punctual as usual. His home was modest. She estimated it to measure about one thousand square feet. It was, however, kept in pristine condition. Very well maintained. The house sat on the front of a large parcel of land that included a very large Tennessee-style barn with a Gambrel roof. She was greeted by an old black lab that could barely walk as she stopped near the house.

She got out of her car just as a man came from inside the house to meet her. "Don't mind old Dude," he said to her. "He's gentle."

Emily reached down to rub the dog's head a little. When she left the dog and moved toward the man, she realized just how bad the dog smelled.

"I'm Tom Dellinger," the man said as he reached to shake Emily's hand.

"Nice to meet you," she replied. "I'm Emily Lane."

Tom was an older gentleman. She thought he might be seventy-five years old. He was of average height and weight but walked a little stooped over. His hair was white, at least what little hair he had. He wore a very neatly trimmed handlebar mustache, which was also white. He spoke with a little gravel in his voice. He reminded her of an old actor she had seen in some classic Western movies. *What was his name?* She thought. She would have to Google it later.

"Come on up to the warehouse and I'll show you around," he said. They walked up to the barn, and he slid open a large sliding door that opened up to a display she hadn't expected. Although clean and painted, the outside of the barn still looked like an old barn. Inside, she saw a huge room with a concrete floor that had been painted. It looked like the floor of some garages she had seen where rich men kept their cars. It was as clean as the hospital floors where she worked. The interior walls were covered in sheetrock and were painted a very pleasing shade of grey. Wagons of all sorts were displayed in the front area of the warehouse. Farther back, she could see an area where all types of machines sat—saws, sanders, planers, and drill presses, along with other items she couldn't identify.

As he led her through the warehouse, he pointed out the different designs he had produced. "This one, I just finished. It's headed for Hollywood."

It was a stagecoach. It was a little smaller than Emily expected. For some reason, they always seemed a little larger on the big screen. She peeked inside. The interior was exquisite. Two bench seats facing each other were covered in high-quality leather. They weren't padded very much, but comfort wasn't exactly the object of the old Western coach. Emily could see that this man was a true craftsman.

He then led her by a replica of an old buckboard wagon. Buckboards were the pickup truck of the 1800s. But a buckboard wouldn't be big enough for what she needed. Then they came to a surrey. The Surrey was typically a two-person vehicle. They were more like the convertible sports cars of their time. Not very practical for Emily's purposes.

When they finally reached the back of the warehouse, Tom led her to a drafting table. "I took the liberty of drawing up these plans yesterday after we talked," he said.

Emily gazed at the drawing, not understanding all the symbols, but she could tell it represented a covered wagon.

"I think this will suit your needs," he said. "It isn't as large as a Conestoga, but two mules can easily pull it."

"How big will it be?" Emily asked.

"The body will measure four feet by twelve feet. With the wheels attached, it will be more like five feet wide, and the tongue will add another eight feet. Do you want rubber wheels?"

Emily replied, "No, I want it to be authentic to the early 1800s. How long will it take you to get it built?"

Tom thought for a moment. "Well, I'll have to order the wheels. It will take a couple of weeks for them to come in. I'd say between four and six weeks." Tom rubbed his chin and thought momentarily, then said, "How's $6500.00 grab you?"

Emily tried not to show the shock she was feeling throughout her body. She frowned a bit, then responded, "Well, it grabs quite a bit. Does that include the canvas top and delivery?"

Tom seemed to be rolling his words around in his mouth a bit before saying: "Well, okay you gotta deal."

"Half now, the rest on delivery?" Emily asked.

"Yessum, that'll be just fine," Tom told her.

Emily wrote him a check, and they signed the paperwork to seal the deal. Tom wrote down Emily's address and phone number and said, "Alright then, I should have it ready for you no later than the end of May."

"Sounds perfect," Emily replied. "I look forward to seeing what you have for me. I really appreciate your doing this for me."

She shook his hand, then turned and walked back to her car. On the drive home, Emily took a mental inventory of what still needed to be done before her trip across time. She had retrieved the relics from the museum already. She now, too, had made arrangements for the mules and the wagon. She also had ordered seeds for planting, essential oils, herbs, and medical supplies. She still needed to see about clothing. She had heard from a friend at church that Tessa Blanch was a seamstress used by many of the young ladies in town who attended the Athenaeum Institute. The institute had once been a school for girls run by the Episcopal Church until the head of the school was dismissed for possible improprieties with one of the students. It was now used, at least by outsiders looking in, as a gathering place for people looking to preserve the history of the Antebellum period. Young ladies would periodically attend parties while wearing handmade "period" dresses. Emily was pretty sure there was more to it all than she imagined, but she didn't care enough to ask. History was Daniel's passion, not hers.

When she got home, she would contact Mrs. Blanch to see about dresses suitable for her to wear on a farm in 1818. She would not, however, be wearing petticoats or other undergarments from that period. She intended to take a lifetime supply of bras and panties with her. She was sure Daniel would also appreciate her bringing him Jockey shorts.

As she drove down Biffle Lane toward her house, she saw a car leaving her driveway as she topped the hill. The little car was heading in her direction. The driver of the car wasn't paying any attention to the car he was approaching. He wore sunglasses and looked straight ahead as he drove, never taking notice of Emily as he sped down Biffle Lane toward the highway. Emily recognized the driver immediately. It was Henry Slater.

"Hello, Hank!" she said out loud to herself. "Did you find what you were looking for?"

Emily pulled into the drive, moving toward the garage. She saw when she pulled in that the garage doors were down. He couldn't have gotten in that way. She pushed the button on the remote hanging from her visor and waited for the garage door to open. She parked and got out of the car, moving over to the truck. She checked the truck bed and saw that everything from the vault was still there. She left the garage and went into the house. When she walked into the den, she saw that the deadbolt on the door was no longer locked. She opened the door and noticed scratches on the latch from where someone had picked the lock. She returned inside and looked around the room to see what might be missing. Her eyes moved to the hearth, and she noticed that the locked chest from the vault was gone. She moved around the house, looking for anything else that might have been taken. Then she went back into the garage entryway where the freezer was. She opened the door and moved around some of the packages of frozen meat. There they were. She wryly smiled as she realized he hadn't found the money. It was all still there.

~~~~~~~~~~~~~~~~~~~~

An hour later, Henry Slater pulled into the driveway of his own residence, anticipating the moment when he would finally get to see the contents of that chest stored in the museum vault for the last thirty years. The chest itself had to be worth at least $500.00, he thought to himself. Whatever was stored inside had to be worth a fortune.

He struggled a bit to unload the chest from the car and carry it inside. He sat the chest down on a chair at his kitchen table, then took out his lock-picking tools. After five minutes of fiddling with the latch, he felt it unlock. Sweat was running down his face and dripping onto the chest as he took a deep breath and then exhaled before lifting the lid of the chest. He smiled from ear to ear as he slowly raised the lid and peeked inside. Suddenly, the color left his face. His smile left his lips. His heart skipped a beat. He nearly fainted but was able to recover. He stood staring into the chest, shaking his head slightly, and then he said out loud, "Oh, Emily! You clever girl."

Hank stared at the large piece of limestone Emily had placed inside the chest. On the rock, she had written with a Magic Marker, "Some Old Junk." Henry flashed back to his last conversation with Emily when he had asked her what she had found inside the chest when she got it home. She had responded, "Oh, yeah. It was just some old junk. Some letters and stuff. Nothing worth much."

CHAPTER 11

April 10, 1818: Two weeks after Daniel arrived back at the Gordon House, the work on the house was completed. Daniel awoke just before daylight. His spirit was restless. He was anxious to hit the trail again and ride toward Grinder's Stand. He got up from his bedroll and began packing his gear for the two-day trip. He knew he would pass right through Sheboss Stand, but he intended to stay only for one night. He wanted to reach Grinder's Stand and get some answers about Meriwether Lewis's death. He took out the note he had found on the body of one of the men that had attacked his friends at Sheboss. He read it again for at least the thirtieth time.

September 3, 1809

Dear Mr. Jagger,

In our last meeting, I mentioned to you that your special services might be needed to eliminate a problem with which I am presently concerned.

I am afraid that the time has come for this concern to be dealt with immediately. Your target is M. Lewis. He should be making his way to Washington at this very moment. My scouts tell me that he will be traveling along the Natchez Trail. It is imperative that you intercept and eliminate him before he reaches Fort Nashboro. He will most likely be carrying documents or ledgers with him. Make sure that you retrieve them and deliver them to me. Enclosed you will find a bank note for fifty dollars. Another fifty will be paid once the task

has been completed. I expect to hear from you once your mission is
accomplished.

God speed to you!

T. J.

Daniel, after having read both the ledger and the journal, knew that they belonged to Meriwether Lewis. The ledger contained information about money that was owed to him by the government. They were expenditures that he was supposed to be reimbursed for while serving as governor of Louisiana. The first journal was his personal thoughts written down. It was *not* the official journal of the Lewis and Clark Expedition. *That* journal had been sent to Washington long ago. It was more of an unofficial description of his journey out west—his partnership with William Clark, his interactions with the Indian tribes along their journey, and his thoughts about his relationships, or lack thereof, with women throughout the years. There was also information about his disagreements with President Jefferson. If this information were to get into the wrong hands, Jefferson might be ruined. There were some circumstances of an illegal nature that could cost the president his place as commander in chief. Bribes and underhanded deals were alleged in the book—the types of things that could get a man killed to prevent him from exposing the leader of the new nation.

The second journal was the official version. That one should have already been published. It was due upon their return from the West but had never been delivered to the president.

Daniel knew there were various theories about Lewis's death. Some believed he had committed suicide after becoming increasingly depressed because of his lack of purpose in life. He had little to do after completing his mission of looking for a passage to the West with his partner, William Clark. He had also failed at love multiple times, failing to ever find a bride with which to spend his life. Others believed he had been robbed and murdered. Statements had been made that the owner of the inn where he was spending the night had heard gunshots just before dawn. When they searched his room, they found him dead, lying on a buffalo rug. He had been shot twice. Once in the head and once in the gut. His throat had also been slashed. Historians over the years have not been able to determine the actual circumstances surrounding his death. Daniel was hoping he could find evidence to support his own theory that he now had developed.

Meriwether Lewis was appointed by Jefferson to serve as governor of Louisiana, but Lewis's request for reimbursement of several expenses he had made while serving as governor had been withheld. Lewis had been told that he would be reimbursed once he had delivered his journal for publication. Although Jefferson no longer held the office of the presidency, he still held considerable control over Lewis. Lewis had become disenchanted with the whole political scene. He was becoming a bit of a troublemaker in the eyes of powerful men serving in Washington. Daniel now knew that Lewis had evidence of improprieties committed by the president himself. Daniel also now believed the letter that was in his possession was written by President Thomas Jefferson. He hoped to substantiate his theory while at Grinder's Stand.

Daniel folded the letter and stuck it inside his shirt pocket. He placed the books inside his saddlebags. He slung two braces over his shoulders, crossing them over his chest. Each brace held one of the pistols he brought back from his adventure at Sheboss Stand. He also draped a powder horn over his shoulder and secured two tomahawks inside his belt. He picked up two rifles and two more powder horns and carried them outside.

Eli, one of the slaves, had brought up two of his horses. Daniel had requested he do so the night before. Daniel swung the saddlebags over Hoss's saddle and tied them down. The other horse, a sorrel with blue eyes, was wearing a pack. Daniel slung one of the rifles onto the pack animal and the other into the saddle that Hoss was wearing. He slung the powder horns over the saddle horn along with his canteen. Miriam, one of the slave women, walked over to Daniel and handed him a small poke containing biscuits and bacon gleaned from the morning's breakfast. Everyone at the camp was well into their workday, even at this early hour. Breakfast would begin for everyone soon, Everyone except Daniel, Gus, and Tom. Gus and Tom knew Daniel would be leaving early, and they would be needed to help him cross the Duck River again. Daniel told Miriam and Eli, "Thanks," and then led his horses to the river.

As Daniel approached the ferry, Gus and Tom were just finishing their work of untying the raft from its secured position.

"Morning, Gus! Tom!" he said as he led his horses onto the ferry raft.

"Mornin'!" they both said in unison. Jake followed the horses as they stepped onto the raft, then proceeded to sniff his way around the raft, looking for nothing in particular. Daniel tied the horses to the side rail and then stood between them to help steady their nerves on the journey across the river.

"Jake, sit!" Daniel commanded.

Jake obeyed and sat down next to the edge of the raft, close enough to see into the water in case something interesting happened to swim by them.

Gus spoke to Tom and said, "Let 'er go, Tom!"

Tom unwrapped the line that had tied the raft on the shore, then jumped on the raft as it eased away from the bank. Tom grabbed the rope on one side of the raft, and Gus took the other side. They worked together, pulling the ferry across the river. Hand over hand, they tugged on the rope that stretched from one bank to the other. Ten minutes later, they reached the far bank of the Duck. Tom walked to the other side of the raft to secure it so Daniel and his companions could disembark. As Daniel and the horses reached dry ground, led by Jake, Daniel turned back to the men and said, "See you, boys, in a week or so."

Gus walked over to Daniel and quietly said, "Now, you be vigilant out there."

"Thanks, Gus. I think I'm a little more ready this time around. I'll be careful."

Daniel and his little caravan ambled down the trail, heading for She-boss Stand. Spring was sprouting. Songs of the mockingbird, blue jay, and many other species could be heard throughout the forest. Dogwood was in bloom. Their white blossoms dotted the green background that surrounded the Natchez Trail. His ride down the trail was peaceful. He allowed himself time for his mind to wander. He thought about Emily. He ached to see her again. It had been such a long time since he had held her in his arms and kissed her. He wondered if they would ever be together again. Then he stopped. *No*! he thought to himself, *I can't allow myself to think that way. I'll see her soon*. Daniel continued his ride, watching the squirrels chase one another through the treetops and scampering along the ground. Jake took an indirect path along the trail, moving from tree to tree, marking his territory along the way. It was a beautiful day for a ride.

About three o'clock that afternoon, Daniel rode into the clearing at Sheboss Stand. From a distance, he saw David working at the corral. Jake ran ahead and met David as he was coming out of the corral. Jake wagged his tail furiously and panted as he moved in circles around David. David saw him and said with delight, "Jake! Good dog!" Then he looked up and saw Daniel riding toward him.

David raised his right hand in greeting and announced, "Daniel! Nafkl!"

Daniel was taken aback for a moment, realizing what David had said. *Nafkl, he thought, that means brother*. Daniel smiled with the realization that David had honored him in this way. He returned the compliment. "David, nafkl!"

Daniel stepped down from his mount and the two men briefly embraced. David asked, "You stay?"

"Only for one night," Daniel answered. "I'm on a journey, so I must leave tomorrow."

David responded, "Good you stay!" David took the lead of Daniel's packhorse and led him to the corral. The two men unpacked the horses and then led them into the corral so they could eat with the other horses.

As the men walked toward the house, David spoke. "Sarah, happy to see you."

Daniel said, "I will be happy to see Sarah, too."

Just as they reached the house, Sarah came lunging from the house. She ran to meet them saying, "Daniel! Oh, its so good to see you! I heard someone ride up, but couldn't tell who it was."

Daniel greeted her, "Hello, Sarah! I'm happy to see you again. How have you been?"

"Oh, we're doing fine. It's been mighty quiet around here the past couple of months. I didn't expect to see you so soon, though. Will you be able to stay for a while?"

Daniel answered, "No, I'm afraid not. I'm on my way to Grinder's Stand. I'll be leaving in the morning."

"Grinder's Stand?" she asked. "Why do you need to go there? Oh, I'm sorry. It's none of my business."

"Oh no!" he said. "It's okay. I've just got some questions about an incident that happened there a few years back. I'm hoping they can clear things up for me. We have a saying in my time. 'Inquiring minds want to know.'"

With a concerned look on her face, Sarah responded. "You be careful there. Those folks aren't as welcoming as you might hope."

Daniel said, "Don't worry. I'll be careful."

Sarah said, "Well, come on in, you two. We'll be eating soon. I hope you're hungry, Daniel."

Daniel smiled and said, "I sure am. My bacon and biscuits left me a long time ago."

Later that evening, they all made their way to the dogtrot where the table was set. Sarah had prepared a meat stew made from squirrel, carrots, and potatoes. They also ate fried cornbread. For dessert, she made a pecan pie. It was all so delicious. Daniel had seconds of the stew and even indulged in eating two pieces of pie.

After supper, Daniel walked back to the corral to check on the horses. He made sure they all had hay and plenty of water for the night. He grabbed his gear and carried it all back to the house. Once he settled into the cabin, he came back out to the dogtrot to enjoy the evening air along with Sarah and David. Jake found a spot in a green patch of grass and wallowed in it like a pig in mud. They all traded stories about their time away from each other over the past two months. Daniel told them about the Gordon House that he had helped finish building while he had been away. As the skies grew dark, they all retreated to their respective rooms to bed down for the night.

The next morning, Daniel woke to the sound of raindrops falling onto the roof of his cabin room. It wasn't a heavy rain. There wasn't any lightning or thunder. It would be a dreary day of riding if it continued all day, but Daniel was determined to get to Grinder's Stand by sunset.

Sarah had breakfast waiting for him as he exited his room. They all ate without speaking. Once they had finished, Daniel said, "Sarah I know you are worried about my going to Grinder's Stand, but this is something I have to do. There is so much about this time in history that has been lost or miswritten. I need to find the answers for myself. I need to do this before its time for me to go back to my time. People in my time know about the Gordon House and the ferry. They know a little about Grinder's Stand. But they don't know much about you and David. They know that Sheboss Stand existed, but they don't know who ran it or where it was located exactly. And they don't know for sure the circumstances surrounding the death of Meriwether Lewis. I want to clear that up if I can."

Sarah said, "I understand, Daniel. But I hope you understand just how dangerous this could be. Those people aren't like us. That stand isn't on Chickasaw land. They built it right next to land held by the Chickasaw nation. They do things their own way. They don't answer to anybody but themselves. If they want you dead, they'll just kill you."

Daniel replied, "I promise I'll be careful. I need you to do one thing for me though."

He reached into his saddlebags and brought out the books. They were now wrapped in a cloth and tied up with a leather string. "These books are very important to me. I need to make sure that they don't fall into the wrong hands. Can you hide them for me?"

Sarah nodded and said, "We will. They'll be waiting right here for you when you come back."

Daniel got up from the table and walked over to Sarah. He hugged her as she stood up to meet him. He reached out and shook David's hand, then walked toward the corral. After repacking the sorrel and saddling Hoss, he mounted up and moved toward the far edge of the clearing, where he found the trail leading west. He turned around in the saddle and waved to his friends, then rode away.

The ride was uneventful. It lightly rained the whole day. He was thankful for the poncho he had bought at Gordon's Trading Post before he left. It was heavy. It had been made from deerskin and still had the hair on it. The hair helped to repel the rain away from his clothing. It also kept the powder in his pistols dry. His buckskin pants, which he now wore instead of his jeans, were also somewhat water-repellent. But since the hair had been removed they didn't completely keep him dry.

At midday, he found two large hickory trees that gave decent shelter from the rain. He stopped to rest the horses and give Jake a breather. The horses found some sparsely growing clumps of grass that they nibbled while Daniel shared his lunch with Jake. After a short rest, he mounted back up, and they continued down the trail heading west.

About four hours later, the clouds parted as the sun broke through, sending the rain away as it did. Shortly afterward, the trail opened up too. Daniel walked his caravan into a clearing that lay to the right of the trail. He had arrived at Grinder's Stand.

It was owned by Robert Evans Griner and his wife, Priscilla Knight Griner. It was originally known as Indian Line Stand because it rested next to land owned by the Chickasaw. It eventually was taken over by the Griners, who named it Griner's Stand, but the people who frequented the place mistakenly called it Grinder's Stand. The name stuck. There were four buildings toward the middle of the clearing. The one farthest away was situated next to a corral. It was a barn that also served as a residence for some of the men who worked at the stand. The next closest building looked to be the residence of the proprietors. Next to it was a cabin with a dogtrot in the middle. It appeared to be for guests who needed a place to stay for the night. Lastly was a rough-looking log structure. There wasn't much of a door. It just sort of hung off to one side. One man was coming out of the structure as Daniel approached. The man could barely stand up. He stumbled along a short path that led to an outhouse. Daniel decided the structure must be a tavern. He decided he could ask about lodging in there.

He tied his horses up at a hitching rail in front of the structure, then cautiously walked to the door opening. He looked down at Jake and said, "Stay!" Jake gave a little whimper but obeyed his new master.

Daniel looked around as he entered. It wasn't what he had expected. It was nothing like the saloons he had seen in movies back home. There weren't a lot of tables spread around the room. Men weren't gathered around a bar drinking whiskey. There were no scantily dressed women. No games of chance. No mirror behind the bar. There wasn't even a bar. There was a long, wide, rough-cut board laying stretched across the back of the room. It was supported by two whiskey barrels. There was only one table, only it wasn't really a table. Another board structure was nailed together and supported by four log legs. The chairs were similarly constructed benches. It was a large table meant to serve several men at one time. There was only one customer inside at the time, standing at the makeshift bar. Another man stood behind the bar, staring at Daniel as he walked in.

"Can I help you, mister?" the man asked.

He spoke with a thin, squeaky voice. He was a small man, clean-shaven and balding.

Daniel responded to his question. "Who might I speak with about a room for the night?"

The barkeeper replied, "That'd be Miss Prissy. She'll be along here before dark. You can talk to her then. Would you like some food or drink in the meanwhile?"

"That sounds good," he replied, then walked around to one end of the table to sit down.

The bartender scooped up a large serving of stew and emptied it onto a tin plate. Then he asked, "You want ale or whiskey?"

Daniel responded, "Ale."

The bartender grabbed a tin mug and held it under the tap of a big wooden barrel, and filled the mug with a light-brown ale. He brought the plate of food and the ale over to Daniel and sat it on the table in front of him. "That'll be four bits," he said.

Daniel reached under his deerskin poncho and found his leather pouch holding his money. He found what he was searching for without seeing it. He then placed a silver dollar on the table. "Can I get an extra plate of food for my dog?" He looked toward the door as he asked the question.

The barkeeper saw Jake sitting beside the door for the first time. He turned back to Daniel, picked up the coin, and said, "This'll take care of it."

Then, he walked back to the bar to collect another plate of food. He brought the extra plate of stew from around the back of the bar and started moving toward the door. As he approached, Jake showed his teeth and snarled at the man. The man stopped dead in his tracks as Daniel called to him, "Mister? You'd better bring me the plate. I'll feed him. He doesn't much like strangers."

The little man slowly backed away from the door and set the plate on the table near Daniel, then retreated back behind the bar as Daniel said, "Thanks!"

Daniel got up from the table, leaving his food and drink temporarily. He carried the extra plate of food and put it in front of Jake and said, "There you go, boy."

Jake quickly gobbled up the food and licked every morsel away from the plate. As Daniel reached down to take the empty plate away, Jake licked his hand in thanks. Daniel rubbed the dog's head quickly then went back inside to finish his own supper.

After finishing his stew, Daniel sat at the table, sipping his ale and observing the two men who remained in the tavern. He heard Jake give a low rumble as another man stumbled into the room. Daniel recognized him as the man he had seen earlier, making his way to the outhouse. The man didn't seem to notice Jake or Daniel as he stumbled back in and made his way to the other end of the table, where he sat down and lowered his head, eventually resting it on the table. Daniel decided he needed to tend to his horses. He looked at the bartender and asked, "Can I take my horses up to that corral and have them looked after?"

The little man responded, "You'll have to wait for Miss Prissy to decide whether or not you can stay."

Daniel thought, *What a peculiar place. Is this an inn or not?* He decided to at least find a patch of grass where they could eat something. He got up from the table and went outside. He had just untied the horses and began to lead them away from the tavern when he noticed a woman walking toward him from the house he had seen before. She was a portly woman, a little older than he, and she had pale blue eyes. She walked with authority. He could tell that she was someone who expected to get her way in all things. As she came to a stop a few feet in front of Daniel, he also noticed that someone had come out of the tavern and was watching them. It was the man Daniel had seen standing at the end of the bar. He was now standing by the door, holding a long rifle. Daniel instinctively moved his right hand underneath his poncho and rested it on one of the pistols he wore.

Priscilla Griner now began asking questions. "What are you lookin' for, mister?"

Daniel replied, "I was hoping to find a place to stay for the night."

Prissy looked at the horses, and Daniel noticed that her eyes were narrowed a bit when she saw the sorrel. "Are these your horses?" she asked.

"They are," Daniel replied.

"That sorrel looks a lot like Jim Jagger's horse."

Daniel remembered the name Jagger from the letter he had found on the dead man's body. Prissy's voice grew a little louder as she demanded, "Where'd you get that horse, mister?"

Daniel responded calmly, "No offense, ma'am but that's none of your business."

Prissy raised her voice another notch and said, "I'm *makin'* it my business. Jim Jagger is a friend of mine and *that's* his horse."

Again, Daniel spoke calmly and said, "I got this horse off a man who along with three other men were attacking a defenseless woman. If that was Jim Jagger, then you need to be more careful about who you pick to be friends with."

Prissy's pale eyes were cutting Daniel now as she more calmly asked, "You killed them? All four? By yourself?"

Daniel said, "I had help."

Prissy began again, "Yeah, I bet it was that dirty no-good Injun, *David Colbert.*"

Daniel's eyes narrowed a bit as he contemplated her statement. Why would she suspect David had anything to do with those killings? Unless she had set up a deal with Jagger and his men to eliminate Sarah and David. But why? Did she think she could take over the stand? There's no way the Chickasaw nation would allow that to happen. Only their people were allowed to operate stands on the Natchez Trail.

Prissy could tell he was thinking things out in his head. She knew now was the time to act. She looked over to the man standing in the doorway and gave him a slight nod of her head. The man raised his rifle to take aim at Daniel's head. He pulled back the hammer, but before he could squeeze the trigger to fire, Jake leaped at the man. He grabbed the man's left arm, which was steadying the rifle. A shot rang out but missed its mark going high above Daniel's head. Jake, snarling and growling, held the man's arm between his teeth. He ripped away at his arm, shaking it like a ragdoll. The man screamed and thrashed trying to free his arm away from the jowls of his attacker.

Daniel was stunned for a moment, having realized just how close he had been to receiving a musket ball to the head. He quickly regained his composure, but it was too late. Prissy brought up a short wooden club she had been concealing behind her skirt in her right hand. She swung it high and hard, catching Daniel in the back of the head and knocking him to the ground. She stood over his body, smirking at him and enjoying the deed she had done.

CHAPTER 12

D aniel lay face down on the ground stunned. His head was bleeding. It pounded and throbbed like pistons moving up and down in an engine. He couldn't see anything but blackness and the stars that danced around in front of him. He gave up and just lay in the dirt. He heard someone yelling from what seemed like a distance. It was Prissy. "Robert! Get out here and get that dog off of Homer!"

The little man who had been tending the bar was her husband, Robert Griner. He came running toward the door with a broom in his hand. He tried to pry Jake away from his prey. He only angered Jake more. Jake turned on Robert and jumped at him. Robert retreated back into the tavern, slamming the broken door behind him. Jake barked at the closed door, then turned to see Prissy standing over Daniel's fallen body. He lunged from the front of the tavern at Prissy, causing her to back away from Daniel. Jake straddled Daniel's body, barking and growling at Prissy while protecting his master from further damage. Prissy tried a few feeble swipes at Jake with her club but never came close to making contact with the dog.

Suddenly, twenty armed men came rushing from the trail. They were all dressed in frontier clothing. All armed to the teeth. They all spread out encircling the tavern and those who were positioned in front of it. Two of the men rushed the doorway, disarming Homer who still lay next to the now closed door. Two more men knocked the closed door off of its leather hinges. Inside, they found Robert crouching with fear behind the bar, and another man passed out at the table.

The leader of the group called out to Prissy as he approached her. "Put : down, Prissy!" he demanded.

Prissy gritted her teeth and yelled back to the man, "You got no call oming in here to my place and telling me what to do!"

The man spoke loudly and with authority as he instructed her, "As ommander of the Tennessee Militia, I've got every call to do whatever is ecessary to keep the peace. Now, drop it!"

Defiantly, Prissy dropped the club and stood still while two more of the nen approached her and bound her hands behind her with leather thongs. The leader then turned around and called out, "Simmons! See what you an do for this man."

An older man with a long white beard came running up from behind he band of men. He looked down at Jake as he hovered over Daniel and eplied, "Yessir, Colonel!"

Simmons slowly and cautiously knelt beside Daniel's body while sooth- ngly speaking to Jake. "It's okay, boy. I ain't gonna hurt him."

Simmons slowly reached his hand forward to allow the dog to sniff him. ake growled but made no attempt to harm the man.

"It's okay, boy. I won't hurt him none."

Jake sensing that the man meant no harm to his master, allowed the man o touch Daniel and see to his wounds. Simmons continued to talk to Jake nd reassure him as he helped Daniel. He reported to the colonel, "Looks ke a pretty good gash here, Colonel. I'll have to stitch him up."

The colonel responded to him, "See to it, Simmons. Once you get him xed up, let's get him bedded down in that cabin over there. You can set it p as a infirmary."

Simmons looked around, finding the cabin, and then responded, Yessir."

The colonel began barking orders to all of the men, "Tanner, get these orses settled in at the corral up there and bring this man's gear down to he infirmary when you're done. Smyth, get Prissy and these men into the

tavern and secure it. It's now the stockade. You four men set up a perimete
around the stand and keep an eye out for hostiles. The rest of you mer
start setting up camp. Put my tent up next to the infirmary. Simmons, onc
you get that man settled in, take a look at Homer's arm. It looks a migh
chewed up."

They brought Daniel into one of the cabin rooms so Simmons coul
sew him up and make him more comfortable. Jake followed along, neve
leaving Daniel's side. They stretched Daniel on his side on top of a table i
the room so Simmons could more easily reach his head when he stitche
him up. Simmons had his orderly, a young man named Johnson, clean u
the wound on the back of Daniel's head with water. Then Simmons cam
in with a needle and hair from a horse's tail that had been soaked in whiske
to stitch up the hole that the club had made. He doused the wound wit
whiskey before he began sewing up the hole. Daniel's body jerked a littl
as the whiskey was applied, but he didn't wake up. Simmons then took
big swig from the jug to steady his hands a bit. As Simmons began pokin
the needle through the skin on Daniel's scalp, he said, "Now, hang in ther
young feller. This might hurt a might, but we'll have you fixed good as ne
before you know it."

Eight stitches later, Simmons wrapped a cotton bandage aroun
Daniel's head, and then he and Johnson moved Daniel onto the bed, layin
him on his side. Jake sat at the side of the bed, keeping watch over h
master.

"Johnson, you stay here and keep watch over him in case he wakes up
Don't let him move around much or he might tear out them stitches."

Johnson nodded to the doctor and began cleaning up the mess they ha
made on the table.

Simmons grabbed his medical kit and left the infirmary, then heade
over to the stockade. Clark was standing guard at the door, and he opene
it for Simmons as he approached the stockade. When he entered the roon
he found Homer sitting at the table, cradling his left arm next to his bod

wincing in pain. Simmons walked over to him and said, "Let's have a look at that, Homer."

Simmons carefully set Homer's arm on the table in front of Homer so he could examine it better. He looked around and saw a lantern at one end of the bar, so he grabbed it and set it down on the table to see better.

"My, my," said Simmons. "That dog sure made a mess of your arm, now. You want me to go ahead and take that arm off for you?"

Homer's eyes doubled in size as he stared at Doc and said, "What? Are you crazy? You can't take my arm! I need it!"

Simmons jokingly responded, "Well, it would probably be a lot less painful for you. You know dog bites ain't nothing to sneeze at. Who knows? Maybe he's got the hydraphoby."

"Hydraphoby!" Homer replied.

"Well, maybe not," said Simmons. "You just never can tell. I tell you what. I'll clean it up best I can and we'll give it a few hours. If you start slobberin' around your mouth or start growlin' at folks though, I'll have to put you down. All right?"

Simmons grabbed the small jug of whiskey from his medical kit and generously poured it onto Homer's arm. Homer cried out in pain as he did so. Then Simmons said, "I won't bother trying to stitch it all up. It's too big of a mess. It'd take me hours to sew you all back up."

Instead, Simmons unrolled a roll of cotton bandage from his kit as he wrapped Homer's arm with the bandage. He secured the bandage by tying the end into a knot.

"There you go," said Simmons. "Now if you feel like you might be comin' down with the hydraphoby, give me a holler, okay?"

Then, with a small chuckle, Simmons packed up his kit and prepared to leave. Just as he started to leave the stockade, he turned and moved around behind the bar to one of the barrels that sat on its side at the end of the bar. He pulled out his small whiskey jug, pulled out its stopper, and held it under the tap of the whiskey barrel. He pulled the tap handle and filled his jug to the top, then put the stopper back in. Then, with a light step and a happy whistle, he left the stockade.

As Simmons made his way back to the infirmary, he was met by the colonel. "Simmons? How are the patients doing?"

Simmons replied, "Fine, colonel. Homer's just got his arm chewed up a bit. As long as that dog in there isn't hydrophobic, he should be okay. As for that young feller in the infirmary, he'll be out a while I imagine. He got a hard wallop on the noggin. I sewed him up to stop the bleedin', but he should be okay."

The colonel responded, "Let me know when he wakes up."

"I'll do 'er, Colonel," Simmons said.

Simmons entered the infirmary to check on Daniel once again. Jake was still sitting by Daniel's bed. Simmons looked at the dog with admiration, thinking he wished he had a loyal dog he could depend on during a scrape. He decided that Jake might be hungry, so he reached into his knapsack and poked around, searching for something to eat. He found some cooked bacon wrapped up in a bit of cloth. He unwrapped the bacon and moved toward Jake. "Here, boy. Are you hungry?"

There were two things Simmons didn't realize about Jake. Unlike most dogs, Jake's eating habits were very peculiar. He only ate when he was hungry, and he only ate food that he had hunted or that Daniel had given him. As Simmons approached the dog with the bacon, Jake turned his head away from Simmons. When Simmons persisted in trying to give Jake the bacon, Jake turned his head away even further. "It's okay, boy. Aren't you hungry?" Jake didn't want to be rude, but he didn't trust this man. He finally got tired of the man, so he showed his teeth and growled at Simmons as a warning.

"All right," said Simmons, "I'll just put it here on the floor for you when you get ready for it."

Simmons checked Daniel's bandage and felt his forehead. Satisfied that Daniel was fine for now, he walked away and prepared himself a bed for he night. Just as he finished settling in his gear, a young man of about eventeen came into the infirmary carrying a plate and a cup.

"Here you are, Doc," said the young man.

"Thanks, Billy," he said. The boy then left the doctor alone with his upper. Simmons prepared to sit down to a plate of beans and a biscuit with a cup of black coffee. Before he sat down, he looked around the room s if someone might be watching him. He reached into his medical kit and rabbed the jug he had recently filled. He uncorked the anti-septic jug and poured a little into his coffee cup. He then replaced the cork and put the ug back into his medical kit. Thirty minutes later, Billy returned to collect he plate and cup. Simmons was already lying on his bed, fast asleep.

The next morning, as the sun began to rise and peek through the infir-nary window, Daniel slowly opened his eyes without lifting his head. He ound himself face-to-face with Jake who was resting his head on the side f the bed, waiting for Daniel to awaken. Daniel smiled a bit, then said, Hello, Jake."

Daniel reached up with his hand and rubbed the dog's ear and the top f his head. Jake responded with a slight *"umph"*. Daniel tried to raise his ead a bit but decided he wasn't quite ready to do so.

Just then, Daniel heard a voice ask, "How ya doin', young feller?"

It was Simmons. He raised up from his own bed as he asked the ques-on.

Daniel replied, "I've been better. My head is pounding, but I guess I'll ve. How long have I been out?"

Simmons said, "Well, we got here just before dusk yesterday and found ou passed out on the ground. So I'd say maybe ten or twelve hours. You're ucky we got here when we did. For some reason, Prissy took a dislikin' to a and bonked you on the noggin."

Daniel asked, "What did she hit me with?"

Simmons responded, "She carries around a short little club that's tied to er wrist with a leather thong. Why she hit you anyways?"

Daniel said, "We were having a discussion about one of my horses. Sh
wanted to know where I got it. Said it belonged to a friend of hers named
Jim Jagger."

"Hmm," said Simmons, "yeah, Jim Jagger is as notorious a scoundrel a
there is. Known for his talent of bushwackin' folks. Is that his horse?"

Daniel responded, "I guess it might have been. If he's the one leading th
gang that attacked my friends at Sheboss Stand."

"You say he might have been. Does that mean he's dead?"

Daniel replied, "He and three others."

Simmons stated, "Well, I can see where Prissy might have been a bit upse
with you, now. Jim was like a brother to her. Maybe, even more, if'n yo
catch my meanin'. She's been tryin' to get her hands on that stand for quit
a while. Don't know why, though. Everybody knows she can't run it a
long as it's on Chickasaw land."

Just then, the colonel stepped into the infirmary. "Simmons?" he saic
"How's your patient?"

"He's fine, Colonel. His head's still poundin', but he'll live I s'pecs."

Daniel saw the man for the first time. He was tall for most men of h
time. About six feet tall. He was a rugged-looking individual. Even thoug
he was dressed like any other frontiersman, he stood out in the crowc
Without taking his eyes off Daniel, the colonel said to Simmons, "Wh
don't you go check on Homer. Give me a chance to talk to this man."

"Yessir, Colonel."

Simmons gathered his medical kit and left the infirmary.

Daniel gazed at the man standing before him and couldn't help bu
think there was something familiar about his face. He decided to try onc
again to raise himself to a sitting position. This time, with much effort, h
succeeded. The colonel took a seat at the table and faced Daniel.

"Excuse me," Daniel said, "did he call you colonel?"

"He did," said the man. "Colonel David Crockett. Duly elected con
mander of the Tennessee Militia."

Daniel's face lit up like a candle as he realized he was sitting in the presence of one of the most famous men in Tennessee's history. Daniel gushed a little as he said, "Colonel Crockett, it is an honor to meet you, sir."

"Well, mister," asked Crockett, "do you have a name?"

"Daniel, sir," he replied.

"Daniel?" asked Crockett. "Daniel what? I know it ain't Boone. I've met Daniel Boone and you ain't him. Boone's a lot older than you. He's nigh on ninety years now."

Daniel was temporarily stunned to learn that Crockett had met Daniel Boone. He managed to shake it off and responded to the question.

"Daniel Lane, sir."

"Well, Daniel Lane. What are you doing here at Grinder's Stand?"

Daniel said, "Well, I came to see the place where Meriwether Lewis died. I wanted to see if I could determine whether he was murdered or if he died at his own hand."

Crockett said, "That happened nine years ago. Why do you care?"

Daniel replied, "I just think that the man served his country well and shouldn't be looked at as some crazy fool that came up here to this stand to kill himself. In one of the statements recorded concerning his death, Prissy was quoted as saying his throat was cut. Why would a man cut his own throat in order to kill himself, then shoot himself in the stomach? I have documents that led me to believe that he was assassinated."

Crockett asked, "Can I see those documents?"

Daniel looked a little uneasy when he replied, "I don't have them with me. I left them with a friend to keep them safe."

Crockett asked, "Well, can you tell me about these documents?"

"One of them was actually a ledger. It was handwritten by Lewis. One was his diary, which recorded his journey in search of the Northwest Passage with Captain Clark. There was also a letter. It was addressed to Mr. Jagger and signed by someone having the initials, T. J. The letter gave instructions to 'eliminate the problem'. It told Jagger that Mr. Lewis would be traveling on the Natchez Trail on his way to Washington."

Crockett asked, "Where did you find this letter?"

Daniel replied, "I took it off of Jagger's body after I killed him."

Then Crockett asked, "And why did you kill him?"

Daniel struggled a little as he said, "He and three other men attacked my friends, Sarah and David Colbert, at Sheboss Stand. Jagger held Sarah with a knife, ready to slice her throat when I came upon them. I had to try to save her. So I drove an ax into his spine. One of his men came from inside the cabin holding a pistol. Jake, my dog, attacked the man, and I ran him through with a spit rod. David came in from the corral where he had killed the other two men. He saw that Jagger was still breathing, so he cut his throat to finish him off."

Crockett asked, "Where do you come from, Mr. Lane?"

"My wife and I live just outside of Columbia."

"Mr. Lane, what do you hope to accomplished by discovering whether or not Meriwether Lewis was assassinated or not? Who do you think ordered this assassination if it indeed was one?"

Daniel thought momentarily, then answered, "Well, I believe that the T. J. that signed the letter was probably Thomas Jefferson."

Crockett asked, "Let's say it was Jefferson. You know he has already resigned the presidency, don't you? In fact, he resigned before Lewis's death. What good would it do to make accusations against one of the greatest men to serve this new nation? He's an old man living out the rest of his life on his farm in Virginia. Who's going to benefit from bringing charges up against the man who is probably already near death's door?"

Daniel replied, "I guess, it wouldn't benefit anyone necessarily. I just wanted to know the truth about the matter if I could find out for myself. I've always enjoyed history and would like to think that the truth about Lewis's death could be told in an accurate way."

Crockett said, "Mr. Lane, the truth and history very rarely coincide with one another."

A knock came from the door. "Enter!" announced Crockett.

The young man named Billy entered the room and said, "Colonel, Doc sent me over to fetch you. He says Prissy wants to talk with you."

Crockett said, "Tell Simmons I'll be there directly."

Billy replied, "Yessir."

He then turned and left the room, closing the door behind him.

Crockett closed his conversation with Daniel, saying, "Think about what I said, Mr. Lane. Is it really worth gettin' yourself killed over? I imagine your wife would think not."

Crockett opened the door without waiting for a reply and left Daniel and the dog behind.

Moments later, the colonel entered the stockade, where he found Prissy, Robert, and Homer sitting at the table. The fourth man, who had been passed out during the whole ordeal, was just now waking. Crockett glanced at the man and asked, "Who is this man and where did he come from?"

Prissy replied, "That's Bob Wright. He's been in here passed out since yesterday."

Bob groggily got up and made a beeline for the door. The guard stopped him from exiting and looked to the colonel for instructions. "Let him go," said the colonel. "He's got nothing to do with this."

The guard let him pass, and Bob unsteadily ran for the outhouse.

Crockett turned back to Prissy and asked, "Simmons said you wanted to talk?"

Prissy replied, "Yeah, I was just wonderin' how long you plan on holdin' us here."

Crockett said, "Well, I guess that depends on Mr. Lane. We'll have to see if he wants to press charges against you three. If he does, then we'll get ya'll moved to Fort Nashboro where you'll be held until you can stand trial."

Prissy asked, "Well when will you know that?"

"Give us an hour or two, 'til he gets to feelin' better. I'll talk to him and see what he says. In the meantime, make yourselves comfortable. You might be with us for quite a while."

With that, the colonel turned and left the stockade.

Crockett made his rounds through the stand, ensuring all the men attended to their assigned duties. Occasionally, he would stop and talk to the men about things other than military duties. The men liked him. He treated them fairly. He looked at them as brothers, not subordinates. Unlike the relationship he shared with his last commanding officer during the Creek Wars. General Andrew Jackson was never pleasant to his men. He was a bloodthirsty tyrant when it came to the enemy. He hated the British for what they had done to him and his family during the revolution. He also hated anyone who allied themselves with the British. During the Creek wars, those allies happened to be the Creek Indians in the Mississippi territory. Crockett and his volunteers served under Jackson during that war and were ordered to kill whole families of the Creek nation. Men, women, and children were all slaughtered. Crockett had no stomach for this type of warfare. But when he and his volunteers tried to leave, Jackson ordered them at gunpoint to return to the camp or suffer execution. This would not be the last time that Crockett and Jackson would disagree about the way Indians should be treated.

Around noon, Crockett returned to the infirmary to check on Daniel. Daniel was now sitting at the table, eating lunch. Jake was sitting beside him on the floor, waiting for any morsel that might hit the floor.

"Well," said Crockett, "I see you're feelin' a bit better."

"Yes," replied Daniel. "My head is still pounding, but I'm not feelin' dizzy anymore."

Crockett sat down at the table opposite Daniel. The young orderly, Bill, sat a plate of food in front of the colonel and a cup of coffee. As they ate, Crockett continued their conversation.

"After lunch maybe you'll feel like talkin' about those folks we're holdin' in the stockade."

"What will happen to them?" asked Daniel.

"That depends on you," said Crockett. "If you press the matter, they will be escorted to Fort Nashboro and held there until they can be tried for attempted murder and conspiracy to commit murder."

Daniel asked, "How long will that take?"

The colonel answered, "It could take a few months. The trip to Nashville could take about a week. Then we'll have to find the magistrate to determine when he can come and hold a trial. We'll have to find a jury and the trial could take a while itself."

Daniel asked, "What happens to them if I don't press charges?"

Crockett was a bit surprised at the question. Most folks wouldn't think twice about pressing charges after being hit over the head with a club. But, he was also relieved to think that they might be able to work things out without a trial. "They'll be set free."

Daniel thought for a moment, then said, "I don't much like the idea of just letting people walk away scot-free for trying to kill me, but I'm afraid I don't have time for a trial. I have to go back home on June 21st."

Crockett responded, "Maybe we could work out some kind of deal."

Daniel asked, "You mean like compensation for my injuries?"

"Yeah!" said Crockett. "We'll ask Prissy to pay you for that clubbing she gave you."

"How much?" asked Daniel.

The colonel thought momentarily, then said, "Well, how's $100 sound to you?"

Daniel knew that $100 in 1818 was quite a sum of money. Daniel replied, "I can live with that."

After he finished his lunch, the colonel left Daniel and walked back to the stockade. Walking through the doorway, he saw Simmons changing the bandage on Homer's arm. He then turned his attention to Prissy and said, "Prissy, this might just be the luckiest day of your life."

Prissy asked, "How's that?"

Crockett replied, "Well, I just had a conversation with Mr. Lane, and he's willing to not press charges against the three of you in exchange for compensation."

Confusingly, she asked, "Compensation? What's that?"

The colonel responded, "Compensation means you'll give him money for what you did to him, and you'll get to go free."

"How much money?" Prissy asked.

"One hundred dollars," announced Crockett.

"A hundred dollars? Are you daft? Well, that'll 'bout clean me out. How are we s'pose to survive on near nothing?"

Crockett then asked, "How do you feel about a neck-tie party? You'd be the guest of honor. We haven't hung a woman in Tennessee yet. You could be the first."

Prissy's hand rose and felt her throat as she contemplated a noose around her neck. Her mouth hung open, and her eyes were as big as silver dollars. She spoke more softly now when she said, "All right. I'll pay it."

She seemed to shrink in stature, realizing what could be if she didn't abide by the terms she had been presented with.

"One more thing," said Crockett, "from now on you're gonna run a legitimate stand. No more robbin' your patrons. No more schemin' against your neighbors either. If anything happens to Sarah and David over at Sheboss, I'll hold you personally responsible. You and your crew will be banished from this territory. We'll ride you out of Tennessee on rails. I'll split the rails myself."

Prissy nodded in agreement as she looked up at the colonel.

The colonel called out, "Clark!" One of the men standing guard outside the door came into the room. "Clark, you and Billy take Prissy over to her

...ouse. She'll need to gather up her compensation fine. Then, bring her ...ack here. Don't let her out of your sight. If she tries anything, shoot her."

The guard nodded his understanding of the orders given to him and ...aid, "Yessir, colonel."

Billy led the way out the door with Prissy following, while Clark brought ...p the rear. The colonel then turned to Robert Griner, owner of the stand, ...nd said, "Robert, I could sure go for an ale right about now."

Robert's face lit up as he responded, "Sure thing, Davy. Comin' right ...p."

Robert walked around the end of the bar, found three tankards, and ...lled them from the tap. He brought them back around to the table, set ...ne in front of the colonel and one in front of Homer, and then sat down ...o enjoy one for himself.

As they all sipped their ale, Crockett said to Robert, "Robert, you've ...otta quit lettin' Prissy get you into trouble. It's time you took charge of ...he place."

"I know, Davy. But it's just easier to go along with her than to be ...crappin' with her all the time."

Then Crockett said, "It's time you started actin' like a man, not a boy. ...ou too, Homer!"

Homer sheepishly looked at the colonel and said, "But, Davy, she pays ...ny wages. I don't much have a choice in the matter."

"What about that mangled arm there," Crockett said, "you think she's ...onna pay for that? She's gonna get you and Robert both killed if you don't ...tart standin' up to her."

Prissy, Clark, and Billy came walking back into the tavern. When she saw ...he three men sitting together, drinking ale and acting as if nothing had ...appened between them all, she lit into Robert.

"Who's payin' for that ale your passing around, Robert?"

Robert sat up straight, cleared his throat, and said with as much author-...ry as possible, "You are!"

Prissy glared at Robert and said, "Mighty bold now that you got all these men to back you up, ain't cha'?"

Robert responded, "Let's just say I found my backbone. You ain't runnin' things no more, Prissy. This time you went too far. From now on, you take care of things at the house and me and Homer will run the stand and the tavern. And another thing... Colonel? Where's the club?"

Crockett turned to Clark and motioned for him to hand Robert, the club they took off of Prissy when they arrived. Clark handed it to Robert and he marched outside with it in hand. He stepped up to the nearest campfire, where some of the men were loitering, and dropped it into the flames. He looked back to the tavern doorway where Prissy, Homer, Clark and Crockett were all watching him. "There," he said, "there'll be no more of that around here."

Crockett and Homer stood, looking at Robert with smiles on their faces. Prissy, on the other hand, was *not* amused. She remembered the sack of coins she was holding in her hand and shoved it at the colonel. Crockett took the money from her and chuckled a bit as Prissy snarled. Then she asked through clenched teeth, "Am I free to go now?"

The colonel said, "Sure, Prissy. But remember to behave yourself from now on."

Prissy stomped away from the men and slammed the door as she entered her house.

Robert smiled and asked the colonel, "Davy, is there anything else I can do for you?"

The colonel said, "Robert, we'll be stayin' here for a few more days until Mr. Lane is able to ride."

"That'll be just fine, Davy. Do you think your men would like some ale tonight with their supper?"

Crockett smiled and said, "I think they would like nothing better."

That night, as the sun began to sink in the western sky, Robert led the way into the camp, and two of the militia rolled a barrel down to the campsite. They set the barrel up on a stump, and Robert hammered a tap into the end of the barrel. Each man brought his tin cup to the barrel and filled it with ale. They all enjoyed the ale, not eating much supper, singing, dancing, and telling stories. As the night skies darkened, Robert rose from where he had been seated and said to Homer, "Homer, would you mind keepin' an eye on the tavern for me tonight?"

Homer squinted an eye as he asked, "Where *you* goin'?"

Robert replied, "I'm gonna sleep in *my* house tonight."

Homer smiled a bit and nodded to Robert as Robert skipped his way back to the house. Robert hadn't slept in his own house in years. He had a small room in the back of the tavern where he slept on a cot. As he entered the house, he discovered that Prissy had already gone to bed. He heard her call from the bedroom, "Who's there?"

Robert walked to the bedroom doorway and said, "It's me, your husband."

Prissy let out a humph and said, "Husband. Well, what do ya want?"

Robert entered the room while holding a lantern he picked up from the sitting area. "I just thought I would sleep in my own bed for a change. Would you like to share my bed with me?"

Prissy looked at him questioningly, then slowly responded, "I guess so."

With a sneaky little smile on his face, Robert stripped down to his night clothes and jumped into the bed. Then, with a *poof*, he blew out the light.

CHAPTER 13

The next few days were uneventful. Some men were sent out on patrol while the rest continued to work around the camp. Daniel spent most of his time sitting in the shade of a hickory tree located on the eastern side of the cabin, which was used as an infirmary. Colonel Crockett wandered around the perimeter of the stand most of the time. The boy named Billy followed him in case the colonel needed to relay a message to the men. Crockett was known for his abilities as a hunter. So, anytime he could steal, a moment away from the men was spent searching for a black bear, deer, or turkey.

Two days later, Daniel was pronounced healed and well enough to travel. The militia packed up the camp and proceeded toward Nashville. Daniel rode along with them as far as Sheboss Stand. He spent a few days with Sarah and David before returning to the Gordon House.

Sarah met Daniel as he rode into the clearing where her cabin was set. She wore a smile on her face as he rode in, but her smile turned to concern when she realized he was slumping a bit in the saddle.

"Daniel! Are you all right?"

"I'm fine," he said. "It seems the Griner's weren't as happy to see me as you are, now."

Sarah asked, "What did they do to you?"

Daniel replied, "Prissy hit me in the back of the head with a club when I wasn't looking. If it hadn't been for the colonel and his men here, I'd probably be dead."

Sarah just realized that the militia was riding into the clearing as well. Her eyes lit up a bit more when she saw the band of men ride up next to Daniel.

"Davy Crockett!" she exclaimed. "How good it is to see you again."

"Howdy, Sarah," he greeted her. "How ya doin'?"

"Oh, we're fine," she answered. "Have your men set up camp anywhere. Will you join us for supper tonight?"

Crockett said, "I'd like nothin' finer." He instructed the men to set up camp and post guards around the perimeter, then stepped down from his horse. David strolled in from the corral to join the conversation as they made small talk. When he arrived, Crockett held out his hand and said, "Good to see you, David. How are you?"

David replied, "Good see you, too."

David then looked at Daniel and said, "Nafkl, good you not dead."

Daniel smiled and replied, "Yeah, I have to agree with you there."

That evening, the four sat around the table under the dogtrot and chewed the fat about the most recent news each could share with the group. They discussed the battle that was presently being fought in Florida between General Jackson and the Seminole Indians. They discussed the admission of Mississippi as a new state to the Union and adopting the new flag. They talked about local news and people who lived in the area. Sarah asked about Davy's family back in Lawrence County. When the sun finally dipped below the trees and extinguished its light, they all said good night and moved to their beds for the night.

The next morning, Colonel Crockett and his militia packed up their camp and readied themselves to continue their trek to Nashville. Before leaving, Crockett sought out Daniel to bid him farewell.

"Mr. Lane, I'm very glad I got to meet you. You are quite an interesting teller. I hope we meet again."

Daniel replied, "Thank you, Colonel Crockett. I have always admire
you from afar, and I am so glad to have met you in person. I regret that m
wife, Emily, could not have met you as well."

The two men shook hands, and then Crockett and his men departec
Sarah asked Daniel quietly as the men marched away, "Does he know wh
you really are?"

Daniel replied while staring at the departing men, "No. I didn't tell hin
I wasn't sure he would have believed me."

"Well, David and I believed you," she said.

"Yeah, well you're kin. Besides, I think the fewer people who know abou
it the better off I'll be."

"How many do know?" she asked.

"You and David, Dolly Gordon, and Gus who runs the ferry for th
Gordons."

Sarah looked a little puzzled as she asked, "Why did you tell Gus?"

"I didn't. He guessed."

Then Sarah asked, "But how would he even know about it? For tha
matter, how would Dolly Gordon know about it unless you told her?"

Daniel thought for a moment before answering her. "What I'm abou
to tell you has to stay a secret. You can tell David if you want, but no on
else." Sarah nodded in agreement.

"Dolly knows about it because Gus told her. Gus knows about it becaus
he's seen 'the shimmering.' Do you remember the story that David tol
that he had heard from the old men of his village?"

Sarah said, "Yes, you mean about the man who came through Ittol
Chuka many years ago. I remember."

"Well," Daniel continued, "the man that was killed many years ago whe
he came through Ittola Chuka wasn't the only one to come through bac
then. He was the only one that the Black Hand saw come through. Ther
was another man that came through that the Black Hand didn't see. Tha
man was Gus."

Sarah stood for a moment in wonder at what she had just been told. Then she said, "You mean that old man came from your world? Your time?"

"Not exactly," said Daniel, "he came through forty-five years earlier than I did. The gateway evidently allows men to travel two hundred years through time. When Gus came through, it was 1973."

Sarah was stunned at the thought of another man being transported through time into her world. How many other people did she meet or know who were from the future? How many others were hiding their true identities? How many had passed through into the future?

Daniel spent the next few days resting and healing from his blow to the head. Finally, he told Sarah it was time for him to go back to the Gordon House. It saddened Sarah to think of him leaving again. She loved talking to Daniel. She loved asking about the future and all of its inventions and the wonders she would never see in her lifetime.

As Daniel was loading his gear onto his horses, Sarah walked out of the house, holding something wrapped in oilcloth. "Here," she said as she handed it to Daniel.

"What's this?" he asked.

"It's your books you asked me to hide. I thought you might want them back."

Daniel took the books wrapped in oilcloth and said, "Thanks. You know, I forgot that I had left them with you. I haven't thought about them in a while, now."

Sarah asked, "Did you find the answers you were looking for about Mr. Lewis's death?"

Daniel shook his head and said, "Naw, Prissy kinda persuaded me to quit asking." He chuckled and smiled as he thought about it. "It just doesn't seem that important to me anymore."

Daniel said goodbye to David and shook his hand. Then he hugged Sarah, and she kissed him on the cheek. "You take care of yourself, you hear?"

Daniel nodded and said, "I hear." He then mounted Hoss and rode away. Jake led the way as they moved down the path that led to the Duck River.

June 19, 1818

The evening shadows were creeping in at the Gordon Place. All the hands had made their way to the camp dining area. Although the house had been finished, there still were no quarters for the slaves or the hired hands, so everyone ate together at the campsite just as they always had. There was one addition to the congregation since Daniel had returned from Grinder's Stand. Lucy Gordon, Dolly's sixteen-year-old daughter, had returned home after spending the last ten months in Nashville, visiting her sisters and their families. Although quiet and somewhat shy around strangers, Lucy was an attractive young woman. Daniel watched her from time to time and thought how different she was from Emily. Emily was always outgoing, confident, and in control. He had never worried that things might not get done around their little farm. Emily always made sure they did. He missed her deeply and yearned for the next days to pass quickly. The summer solstice was at hand, and he, if everything went as planned, would be reunited with his bride very soon.

After supper, Daniel and Gus retired to Daniel's tent to talk. This had become the nightly routine for them ever since Daniel had returned. Gus was full of questions about the future he had missed out on. Daniel had tried to fill him in on what had become of some of Gus' favorite bands, movie stars, and even politicians.

Gus wasn't a bit shocked to learn that Richard Nixon had been impeached shortly after Gus had walked through the Shimmering. Gus wasn't a huge sports fan, so they talked very little about sports figures. Tonight, Gus asked about new inventions. Daniel told him, "Well let's see. Not too long after you left, someone invented the microwave oven."

"What's that do?" asked Gus.

"It cooks your food really fast. You can just heat up leftovers in a couple of minutes, or you can cook a bag of popcorn, or even bake a cake."

Gus asked, "What else?"

"Did you have a television on your place in Summertown?"

Gus replied, "Yeah we used to watch the news on it every night. But it was only a black-and-white TV, and it was small, about nineteen inches."

"Well, TVs have come a long way since then. Your old TV was a CRT or cathode-ray tube, right? Well, they build them with LEDs now or light-emitting diodes. They use transistors and capacitors, and they've done away with the old vacuum tubes. The screens are anywhere from twenty inches to over one hundred inches in size. The picture screens are flat, and the pictures they produce are so crisp and sharp that you feel like you could reach out and touch the people you see on the screen. The TV I have at home is sixty inches, but I've seen some even bigger.

"In the eighties, they came out with a box you could hook up to the TV and watch movies from. It was called a VCR or videocassette recorder. Not only could you buy or rent movies or other programs to watch on it, you could record programs that were being broadcast on the TV so if you couldn't be home to watch it live, you could save it for later. Later on, they replaced the VCR with a DVD player. The digital video disc player played programs on a disk. It held more information than the cassettes and the picture quality was better. They then came out with a DVR or digital video recorder. When you hook it up to your TV, you can record more than one program from what's being broadcasted, and you can even pause live TV. So if you get a phone call while you're watching TV and don't want to miss your show, you just pause it and then finish watching after you han up the phone."

"Wow!" said Gus. "That's amazing! What else?"

"Well, you've heard about computers haven't you? They were around i the 40s, but a computer back then filled a whole room. In the late seventie: people started making them smaller. In the 80s, they actually startin building computers that would fit in a person's home office. They reall took off in the 90s, and then some people got the idea to connect them a together through a system called the internet. Things really took off ther You can get the answer to any question you have about just about anythin in a matter of seconds by using the internet. The computers got smalle and smaller as time went by. Most people use what's called a laptop. It' about as big as one of your old three ring binder notebooks from schoo Some people use an electronic tablet instead. But this is the kicker. Whe the telephone changed, the whole world changed. Aside from businesse and a few old-timers who can't seem to let go of them, no one uses the ol landline telephone."

Gus stared at Daniel like a child hearing a bedtime story for the first tim "What do they use?" he asked.

"Remember some of the old movies where rich people had a telephon in their car?"

"Yeah!" said Gus. "Double Oh Seven had one, didn't he?"

Daniel continued, "Well, they don't put them in cars anymore. Peopl carry them around in their pockets. They fit right in the palm of your hanc and you don't just make phone calls with them. They're small computer: You can call anyone from any part of the world. You can actually video cha with them if you want, so you can see their face, and they can see your The phones have cameras in them, so you can take photos or even videc with them. You can also find your way when you get lost by accessing GPS signal. It pulls up a map, you tell it where you want to go. It alread knows where you are, and it points you in the right direction, at least, most of the time, it does."

Gus started to get a little skeptical, now. "Daniel, are you joshing me?"

Daniel smiled at the question and reached for his saddlebags. He rummaged around a bit and pulled his hand out. He opened his hand to show Gus the cell phone he had brought with him. "This is my cell phone. It doesn't have much power left, but I turned it off when I realized I wasn't going to be able to use it here. So it should be able to at least come on." Daniel pushed the power button on the side of the phone and waited a moment for it to reboot. Suddenly, the screen lit up and came to life right in front of Gus' eyes.

He stared in amazement. "Wow!"

Daniel then told him, "Of course, we won't be able to call anyone, but we can take a picture." He pointed the back of the phone at Gus and snapped a picture. He then turned the phone around and showed it to Gus.

"Is that me? I can't believe it. I haven't seen a clear image of my face in many years, just my reflection in that old muddy Duck."

"Here," said Daniel. "Come over here next to me and we'll take a picture together."

Gus moved over and sat next to Daniel. Daniel put his left arm around Gus while holding the phone in his right hand. He redirected the lens so they could see their image on the phone's screen as they sat there next to each other. Daniel snapped a picture. Then he pulled up the image and showed it to Gus. "This is what we call a selfie. It's a picture of yourself."

Gus teared up a little as he said, "I can't believe it! I've missed so much! That's quicker than a Polaroid picture."

The two continued discussing how the world had changed in the last forty-five years, and then Gus got quiet. "Daniel? When you go back in a couple of days, do you think I could go back with you?"

Daniel replied, "Well, I don't see why not. Where would you go, though? What would you do?"

Gus teared up again and said, "I want to go back to Summertown. I'd like to see if maybe my folks are still alive. I've missed them."

Daniel said, "Well, I know that the Grove still exists there. But, I have no idea if your folks are still alive or if they still live on the Grove. But I can understand your wanting to find them if you can. I've only been away from Emily for six months. I can't imagine being away for forty-five years. I'll take you with me. We'll drive up to Summertown and see if we can find your family."

CHAPTER 14

June 19, 2018: The sun rose early over Emily and Daniel's little farm in Hampshire, Tennessee. The sunlight broke through the glass panes on the French doors in Emily's bedroom at 5:30 a.m. It didn't wake her, though. She had been awake for at least an hour, lying in bed with her mind racing about things she needed to do to prepare for her trek into the past. The mules and wagon had been delivered weeks ago. She had been working with the team, getting used to driving them. She had started by having them pull a sled she had constructed out of logs and scrap lumber around the farm. She would stand on the sled, barking orders to the mules while holding onto the reins. Her closer neighbors, who were only five hundred yards away, could hear her calling out, "Haw, Pepper! Haw, Rusty!" as the mules made a slight left turn. Or "Gee, Rusty! Gee, Pepper!" for a right turn.

Eventually, she worked up the courage to hitch them to the wagon. She could be seen driving the team up and down Biffle Lane. She and the mules quickly became a good team. It was like they knew what she wanted them to do before she told them. Emily was jubilated at the progress they had made.

She had also been working with Tommy Brown on the rifle range in Maury County, learning to load, aim, and fire the muzzle-load guns she retrieved from the Davy Crockett Museum vault. The ear-piercing report the Kentucky long rifles made was difficult for her to get used to. They also gave quite a kick, which bruised her shoulder at first. She eventually learned how to hold the rifle to her shoulder with the right amount of pressure to absorb the recoil rather than receiving a jolt to her body when she squeezed the trigger.

She had steadily been on the internet, learning things like how to make gunpowder and soap, how pioneers stored food for the winter months, and, of course, everything about pioneer medicine she could find. She stocked up on medical supplies and books that would help her get through most any medical emergency, barring open-heart surgery.

Emily had sold off much of the livestock she and Daniel had raised over the years. She kept six pullets that would be raised to be laying hens and a young rooster. She kept one young boar and two gilts. The pigs were six weeks old when she sold off the rest of the herd last week, so they were still small enough to easily be transported on her journey. She kept the mare and her colt. She kept one doe from her goat herd and one buck. Jinks the cat would remain to fend off the rodents in the barn and on the farm for the new owner after she was gone.

She sold her car but kept the pickup truck for now. She would need it to help her get her gear transported to the Trace. She talked to her neighbor Frank Lovell about helping her move everything to the Trace when the time came. He had a flatbed trailer and a large livestock trailer they would be using. The stock trailer would hold the horses, mules, goats, and crates containing the pullets and pigs. They would haul her wagon on the back of the flatbed trailer. In exchange for his help, she would sign over the title of her truck to him. He had no idea what this trip was about. He didn't know he would never see his young friends again. He was simply doing what he could to help Emily out.

Emily finally managed to wrestle herself out of bed to start the day. Just two more days until she would finally be reunited with Daniel. The anticipation was killing her. She had just a few last details to cover before she left 2018 forever. She walked down to the barn and checked all the stock. Everyone was doing fine. There were no more eggs to collect. The pullets would not start laying for another month or so. She *did* milk the doe. The young pigs were no longer kept in the pasture. They had been caught up when the rest of the herd was sold and placed in a stall inside the barn. The horses and mules were content with grazing in their little pasture behind the barn. Once she was satisfied everyone and everything would be fine for the day, she returned to the house, where she showered and dressed for the day's events.

She felt a strong urge to see her family one last time with only two days left. After fixing a large travel mug filled with coffee, she got into the truck and drove to Lawrenceburg to visit her grandpa and aunt for the last time.

As Emily drove down Biffle Lane, she turned on the radio in her truck. It was tuned to a classic rock station in Nashville. Suddenly, she felt nervous in the pit of her stomach. She thought, *"This might be the last time I hear music like this for the rest of my life."*

There were a lot of things that she would never do again. She began to contemplate them all. She would never have a hot shower. She would never cook with a microwave oven. She would never watch Netflix or anything else on TV. She would never drive a car. She would never have the answers to any questions at the tips of her fingers using Google. She would never fly in an airplane again. She would probably never see the beach again. She could never talk to her family on a cell phone again. Then it hit her. She would never talk to her family in Lawrenceburg ever again. This made her tear up. She sniffled, wiped her eyes, and said, "*They won't be around much longer anyway, Emily. As long as you have Daniel, nothing else matters.*"

Forty minutes after leaving, Emily arrived at her grandpa's home. She walked through the carport and knocked on the back door before opening the door and entering. Aunt Linda heard the knock in the kitchen but couldn't get to the door before it opened. Emily called out as she opened the door, "Hey!"

Linda seemed slightly startled until she realized Emily was coming through the door. "Oh, hey, Em'ly. I wasn't sure who that might be. Come own in."

"Whatcha doing?" Emily asked.

"Oh, I'm just finishing up with the breakfast dishes."

"Where's Grandpa?" Emily asked.

Linda replied, "Probly in his study. Go own in. He'll won't to know yor here."

Emily passed through the hallway and entered her grandpa's study, where she found him sitting in his desk chair, half asleep. "Hey, Grandpa!" she called out.

Wild Bill Crockett jumped slightly as he awoke and cheerfully responded, "Emily! Come own in girl. It's good to see ya."

"How are you doing, Grandpa?"

"Oh, fair ta middlin," he said.

They talked for quite a while about local news, his getting old, and Aunt Linda always getting on his nerves. Finally, Emily broached the subject at hand.

"Grandpa, you know what the date is today?"

He thought for a moment, then responded, "Well, no. Not really. What day is it?"

"Today is June nineteenth," she answered. "The day after tomorrow I will be leaving."

"Hmm?" he questioned. "Where will you be going?"

Uneasily, Emily replied, "I'm going to find Daniel, Grandpa. The twenty-first is the summer solstice. That's the day that the gateway opens up so I can get to him. Remember?"

Her grandpa thought momentarily, then asked, "When will you be back?"

Emily hesitated, then said, "Grandpa, I won't be coming back. I'm going to live with Daniel wherever he is now. Remember the letter I wrote that was in the little chest? I decided to leave 2018 and go to live with Daniel in 1818."

CHAPTER 15

June 21, 2018: Emily awoke early before daybreak. She slept very little during the night. The anticipation of what was about to come to pass rattled around in her brain most of the night. She kept going over and over the list in her mind of what she needed to do, what she needed to bring, and how she would accomplish it all.

She took what she knew would probably be the last hot shower she would ever have. She lingered as the hot water ran down her body, soothing and cleaning her skin. When her fingers began to shrivel from long exposure to the water, she finally cut off the water and dried herself. She dressed in her usual T-shirt and blue jeans. There was no need for her to don her dress until it was absolutely necessary; blue jeans would be more practical for the task at hand.

Her neighbor, Frank Lovell, had agreed to meet her early in the morning to help her load the mules and horses into the trailer. The goats, pigs, and chickens had already been packed and loaded late last evening to make things go quicker this morning. All of the gear, including the wagon, was also loaded on the flatbed trailer. Frank and his nephew, Luke, arrived just before five o'clock. Luke would drive Emily's truck back from the Trace once they had unloaded everything. Frank asked Emily, "Well, are you ready to go?"

Emily looked at him and said, "Yeah, let's get this show on the road."

Frank backed his truck up to the flatbed trailer, and Luke backed Emily's truck up to the stock trailer. They got them both hooked up and secured and then they walked up to the barn to retrieve the horses and mules. The mare was waiting for Emily at the barn as she walked in. Emily took a lead rein from the wall of the barn and connected it to the mare's halter. She handed Luke the lead temporarily as she grabbed another lead, walked out into the pasture, and called her mules. "Pepper! Rusty!"

Both mules walked quickly toward Emily and allowed her to rub their muzzles. Emily attached the lead to Rusty's halter, then led him over to Frank and handed him the lead. She grabbed the last lead and attached it to Pepper's halter. Then, she led Pepper through the barn and down through the pasture toward the awaiting trailer. Frank and Luke followed behind, each leading his animal along the way. The mare's colt followed close behind, never straying far from his mother. Once they reached the trailer, all the animals were loaded.

Emily remembered one last thing she needed before leaving. "I'll be right back," she said. She ran back into the house and went to the freezer. She rummaged through all the packs of meat stacked inside until she found what she was looking for. One by one, she removed the bags of gold and silver coins she had hidden in there months ago. Five bags of coins, each holding about one hundred dollars. She placed them in a crate waiting in the garage, then called Luke over to help her. She and Luke each grabbed an end of the crate and carried it out to the flatbed trailer. "This needs to go into the back of the wagon," she instructed.

"What is it?" asked Frank.

"Oh, just a little pocket change," she replied. "Never know when it might come in handy. Luke, would you mind driving my truck?" she asked. "I need to talk with Frank."

Luke nodded, then proceeded to get into the truck. Frank and Emily got into his truck, and he started the engine. As they drove out of the driveway, Emily took a last look at what had been her home for the past few years. She would miss it. But her real home would be wherever she and Daniel were together. *We're gonna live life simpler and live it to the fullest*, she thought to herself.

Once they hit the highway, Emily began to tell Frank her plans—not all of them, of course—but enough to help him understand.

"Frank, I appreciate everything you have done for Daniel and me. You've been a good friend to us over the years."

Frank responded, "Awe, it's nothin'. You and Daniel have been like family to us."

Emily continued, "I won't be coming back, Frank. I'm going to meet Daniel, and we will be living somewhere else. You won't be hearing from us again."

Frank said, "Well, I'm sorry to hear that, Emily. We're gonna miss you two somethin' awful. Are you gonna sell your farm?"

"No," she said. "I've instructed my lawyer to write up a quick claim deed and have it ready for you to sign today."

"Me? What do you mean?"

Emily continued, "We're leaving the farm to you. After all, it was in your family before we bought it from your aunt. It's only right that it should go back to your family. You'll be getting a call from Mr. Samuels today, and he'll instruct you where to meet him."

Frank thought momentarily, then asked, "Well what should I do with it? I've already got a house. I don't need another one."

Emily said, "What about Luke and his new bride? Aren't they living with you? Isn't Luke working for you now? Let them move into the house. It will make a nice new home for them and you and Shirley can go back to being empty nesters."

Frank was silent for a while, then finally said, "Are you sure you won't be comin' back? Where will you live?"

"We won't be back," she said. "And I'll live wherever Daniel takes me."

After driving for forty-five minutes, they pulled into the parking lot at Shady Grove. Emily was a little surprised to see another vehicle in the parking lot. As they drove up and

parked, a tall, slender man got out of the car. "Tommy!" Emily exclaimed.

She got out of the truck, walked over to Tommy Brown, and said, "What are you doing here?"

Tommy shrugged his shoulders and looked at the ground as he said, "Well, I just couldn't let you go off out there by yourself. I thought I might watch your back. You never know what might happen. Sides, there ain't nothin' really holdin' me here noways."

Emily smiled, then wrapped her arms around him and said, "I appreciate your concern for me. If you're sure you want to go, I won't stop you."

The four of them quickly unloaded the trailers and hitched up the mules to the wagon. They tied the mare to the back of the wagon, and then Emily and Tommy climbed into the wagon seat. Emily took the reins and said one last goodbye to Frank and Luke before instructing the mules to move forward. "Get up, Rusty! Get up, Pepper!"

The mules pulled against the wagon's weight and easily hauled it down the road. Emily drove them across the Natchez Trace Highway and into the grounds of the Gordon House exhibit. The sun was just rising over the tops of the trees that encircled the exhibit grounds. They drove past the Gordon House and into an empty field that lay just to the east of the house. They were now out of sight of the Shady Grove parking lot, but something told Emily to turn around and look behind her.

"What is it?" asked Tommy.

"I don't know," she answered. "I've just got the feeling we're being watched."

About two hundred yards to the west, a short, stubby man was hiding in the trees. He wore a blue windbreaker jacket, hiking boots, and a Tennessee Titans ball cap on his fat little head with his ponytail sticking out of the back. The man took out a small pair of binoculars from a fanny pack he wore around his waist. He raised the binoculars to his face and peered through them, looking directly at Emily and her convoy.

When Emily looked back over her shoulder, she saw it. "There! Did you see that Tommy?"

"No. What?" he replied.

"Way back in that tree line. There was a flash of light. Someone is watching us. They're using binoculars. The sunlight is reflecting off of the lenses."

She pulled up the mules to stop. Then looked back again. "There it is again!" she exclaimed.

"I seen it!" said Tommy. "Who do you think it is?"

Emily said, "I'm afraid I know exactly who it is. I knew I shouldn't have shown him the letter. I even warned myself not to. It's got to be Hank Slater."

Tommy asked, "You mean that there museum guy from Lawrenceburg?"

"Yeah, that's him. He tried to steal something from me a couple of days after I showed him that letter. I think he's after the money I've got hidden in a crate in back of the wagon."

Tommy said, "Well maybe we better get movin'."

"Get up mules!" Emily called as she pushed them toward the line of trees about seventy-five yards ahead of them. Emily hoped the Shimmering would expose itself to them as they reached the edge of the field. "Do you see it anywhere?" she asked Tommy.

"Naw, not yet."

They scanned the trees as the wagon moved forward slowly. "It's gotta be here! This is where Daniel's footprints ended when we searched for him, isn't it?"

Tommy replied, "Yeah, but maybe its a little farther into the trees."

They both strained their eyes, searching for the gateway. Emily started to doubt herself. What if it wasn't true? What if it was all just a cruel joke someone was playing on her? What if she would never get to see Daniel again?

Suddenly, it appeared about twenty yards past the tree line, directly in front of them. The sun had finally made it past the tops of the trees, allowing its rays to trigger the opening of the shimmering gateway. Emily gasped. "There it is!"

Tommy followed her finger as it pointed to the Shimmering. Emily asked, "Can we get this wagon through there?"

Tommy replied, "It'll be tight, but I think we can make it."

Emily pushed the mules a little harder as if she thought the Shimmering might disappear before they had time to make it through. The terrain was rough because of old tree stumps and rocks in their path. However, the mules made light work of it as they pulled straight for the gateway. The sun's light reflected off the gateway, causing it to look like a hazy curtain hanging before them. Emily braced herself, expecting the mules to balk at the light dancing before them, but they moved on as if they couldn't see it.

Finally, they broke through. When they did, everything changed. A warm, sunny morning suddenly turned to a dark, cloudy haze. A light rain was falling from the sky. They heard thunder from far away and saw lightning flash off in the distance. Emily saw the open field sprawled in front of them. It tempted her, invited her even to drive into the clearing. She looked around. Trees were standing on both sides of her and her wagon. The left side was a little more sparse in its growth, so she chose it.

"Haw, Rusty! Haw, Pepper!"

The mules turned left and moved farther into the trees. As they made the turn, Tommy said, "Look!"

He pointed back through the open field. Fifty yards away, Emily saw six men on horseback. She couldn't determine who they were, but she felt bad about them.

"Yah! Get up, mules!" she shouted as she returned to her team. Tommy turned back and looked through the tunnel created by the wagon's covering. He could see the men riding quickly toward them. "They're gaining on us!" he cried.

Emily looked over her left shoulder just in time to see Hank Slater moving into the clearing as he ran through the Shimmering. Hank Slater froze as he saw the six men riding toward him. They were all naked from the waist up. Their faces were painted bright red with white stripes crossing their faces, over their noses, from ear to ear. Their hands were all painted black, from their fingertips to their elbows. The man riding in the lead raised his lance and cried out with a bloodcurdling scream as he flung his spear at Hank. With his eyes spread wide in terror, all Hank could do was say, "Oh crap!"

The spear hit its mark. Hank stood momentarily, looking down at the projectile protruding from his chest. It had hit him with so much power that two feet of the lance stuck out Hank's back. Slowly, Hank's knees buckled, and he fell to the ground. Blood flowed from his wounds and his mouth and nose.

He gasped for air, but it failed to enter his lungs because they were filled with blood. Emily's eyes watered as she continued to drive the mules forward. She thought, "*If I hadn't shown him that letter, he'd still be alive.*" She brushed the thought away from her mind and kept driving. Tommy then said, "Looks like they're turning back." The six painted men rode away while singing, "Hoop, hoop, hoop!" as they headed back to the other side of the clearing.

The wagon bumped along the makeshift path. Emily wondered if the wheels might fall off before they reached their destination. She thought, "*The potholes on I-440 in Nashville have nothing on this little trail.*" Slowly, they moved forward until she finally could just make out an opening into a clearing. As she neared the clearing, she heard Tommy say, "Look up ahead."

He pointed toward three horses and a dog coming directly toward them. Two of the horses carried riders, and the other carried a pack. Emily gasped as she squinted to see past the rain that had picked up in volume. Even from a distance, she recognized the tall man riding the big bay stud. It was her, Daniel.

As he rode up, Daniel was curious about who was driving a wagon from the Indian burial grounds. Emily pulled up on the reins to halt the mules, then threw the reins to Tommy as she jumped down from the wagon. When she started running toward Daniel, he finally realized his wife was the woman running toward him in blue jeans and a T-shirt. Daniel dismounted the Bay and ran to meet her. As they met each other in the open field, they embraced each other. Emily kissed Daniel on his face, lips, and neck— whatever part of him in her reach as they seemed to wrestle with one another. Once things settled down, they stood and held each other in the drizzling rain.

Finally, Daniel asked, "What are you doing here? How did you even know how to find me? I was on my way home."

Emily explained, "I received a letter explaining where you were. It didn't give any details other than, I would be able to find you on the solstice at the place where your footprints ended when I searched for you six months ago."

Daniel asked, "How did you get through without encountering the Black Hand?"

"I had learned enough to know not to go into the burial grounds. As soon as we came through the Shimmering, we made a left turn and headed away from them."

Then Daniel asked, "We?"

Emily walked him to the wagon and said, "Daniel, this is Tommy Brown. He is, or *was* a park ranger on the Natchez Trace. When you went missing, he's the one who helped me search for you. He's been a good friend and a big help ever since."

Then Daniel asked, "Well what's with the wagon and the mules?"

Emily explained, "I came to stay. We're going to make a life for ourselves right here. We're gonna live a simpler life and live it to the fullest."

Daniel smiled as he recognized that she was quoting him. "But I was coming home to you. You didn't have to do all of this. Gus and I were on our way."

Emily then asked, "What were you going home to? A job you hated? A lifestyle that you weren't happy living? I know you, Daniel. The only reason you were coming back was because I was there. Well, now I'm here, and you don't have to go back."

Daniel asked, "Are you sure? What about your job?"

Emily replied, "I'm a caretaker. I can do that anywhere I go. I imagine a lot of folks here could use my knowledge in medical care, so I'll do that right here as I'm needed. Otherwise, you and I can set up a farm somewhere and live that simple life you've always dreamed about."

Daniel then remembered Gus was waiting. Daniel escorted Emily over to meet him.

"Emily, this is Gus. He was going back home too. Only he's been gone a lot longer than I was. He came through in 1973."

Emily exclaimed, "Oh my! Where were you from?"

Gus replied, "I lived in a sort of commune in Summertown."

Emily replied, "You mean you were from the Grove?"

Gus was surprised to hear her call it that. "Yes, ma'am, I was. Do you know if it's still there?"

Emily answered, "It's still there, but I doubt that you would recognize it, or that they would recognize you."

Gus said, "I haven't seen my mother or father in over forty-five years. I didn't know it was possible for me to get back there. I wasn't even sure how I got here in the first place, until Daniel figured it out."

Daniel asked him, "Do you still want to go? I'm staying here."

Gus replied, "If it's all the same to you, I'd still like to see if my folks are still alive."

Daniel said, "Then we'll see to it that you make it through safely."

Daniel checked his two pistols to ensure they were ready to be fired, then took two rifles from the horses. Gus got down from the horse he had been riding and unloaded his gear from the horse. They all walked back to the wagon, and Daniel looked up to Tommy and said, "So, you're a park ranger. I know you've been trained to handle firearms. Can you shoot a muzzle-loader?"

Emily interrupted and said, "He taught me!"

Daniel then said, "Well, all right." He started to hand one of the rifles up to Tommy, but Tommy grabbed two rifles from the back of the wagon and checked their loads. Daniel looked at his bride and smiled and said, "Came prepared, did we?"

Emily replied, "Have you ever known me to not be prepared?"

As they started to walk back to the Shimmering, Daniel asked Gus, "Don't you want to take that horse with you?"

Gus said, "No, from what you've told me about 2018, I won't need a horse. But you'll need all the horses you can get around here."

They secured all of the horses and the mules, and then the four of them trekked back through the forest toward the Indian burial grounds. When they got within sight of the clearing, Daniel pulled up. "Who's that?"

"Oh," said Emily, "I forgot to tell you about him. That was Hank Slater. He was the curator of the David Crockett Museum. He used to be a friend of Grandpa's until he double-crossed me. He was after my gold and silver that Grandpa had given me. He evidently tried to sneak through the Shimmering behind us, but the Indians had their own ideas about that."

Daniel looked around at his companions and said, "Okay, is everybody ready?"

"Wait!" said Emily. "Gus, how are you going to get home?"

Gus thought momentarily, then said, "I guess, I'll have to walk."

Emily instructed him, "After you walk through the Shimmering, walk back in the direction we just came from. You'll see the Gordon House is still standing. It's an exhibit, now. There will be a parking lot just the other side of it. Go up there and wait for someone to come along. There's a public restroom there, so people stop there all the time. Get someone to call the Ranger Station. Have them send someone to help you. It will probably be Matthew Douglas. Make up a story about how you got there and that you're just trying to get back home. Don't tell him or anyone where the gateway is. They might decide to put you in a mental hospital if you start talking about time travel. Just act like you belong there. Don't look surprised by anything new that you see. You'll be okay."

Gus nodded with understanding.

Daniel then said, "Okay, let's do this. Gus, leave your weapons here. You won't need them."

Gus handed them over to Emily, then took a deep breath. They walked quietly toward the gateway, scanning the open field for signs that the Black Hand was still there. Daniel, Tommy, and Emily stayed within the tree line along with Jake, who whimpered a little when they stopped.

"Hush, Jake!" Daniel whispered toward the dog.

Daniel motioned for Gus to walk on through to the Shimmering. Gus moved as quietly as he could, looking over his shoulder toward the open field as much as possible without tripping over the ground cover. When he reached the gateway, he looked back at his friends, waved, then flung himself through.

The Black Hand never came back. As Daniel, Emily, and Tommy turned to go back to the wagon, Emily asked, "What do we do about Hank?"

Daniel looked at the body that lay before them on the ground, then suggested, "I guess we could carry him back to the Gordon place. They have a cemetery there. That's where we buried Jimbo."

Emily then realized she hadn't asked about Jimmy yet. "How did Jimmy die?"

Daniel responded, "Pretty much like this poor guy. Only it was farther out in the clearing. It happened before I had come through the gateway. The Black Hand killed him, stole his horse, then left."

Emily quietly responded, "How horrible for him."

Then Daniel said, "Well, if we're going to move him out of here, we're gonna need to get that lance out of him."

Daniel took a tomahawk that he wore inside his belt and chopped off the head of the spear. He then grabbed the end of the spear with both hands while bracing against Hank's chest with his left foot and pulled the spear from Hank's body. He then handed Emily his rifles. He bent down, picked Hank's body up, and rolled it onto his shoulder like a fireman might carry someone from a burning building. Emily and Tommy followed Daniel back to the wagon and the animals through the forest.

Daniel slung the body over the saddle of the horse Gus had been riding, then tied it down with some leather laces he had. He turned to Emily and asked, "Are you ready?"

Emily replied, "Let's go."

They all mounted and rode toward the Gordon House through the open field.

After a thirty-minute ride, they found themselves at the edge of Gordon Place. Emily and Tommy admired the newly built house that stood before them. They were very familiar with the structure, but only after it had been restored from years of wear and tear. To see it brand new was a treat for them both.

Mrs. Gordon came outside as soon as she heard the wagon pull up. She had a concerned look on her face. "Daniel!" she called to him. "I thought you were going home."

Daniel replied, "Well, it seems my wife had other ideas. Dolly Gordon, meet Emily Lane."

"Pleased to meet you, Emily."

Dolly turned back to Daniel and said, "Daniel, I don't mean to be rude, but David was just here looking for you. He rode all night to get here trying to catch you before you went...home."

Daniel asked, "Why? What did he want?"

"He said that his uncle, Chief William was traveling through the area and became ill. He's in poor condition. Sarah sent David here to fetch you. She thought maybe you could help him."

Emily asked, "Did he say what his symptoms were?"

Dolly replied, "No, just that he wasn't doing well at all."

Emily sprung into action. "Tommy, can you help me get my medical gear out of the wagon?"

Tommy crawled into the back of the wagon and searched for the trunk holding the medical supplies. Tommy brought the trunk to the back of the wagon and opened it for Emily. Emily rummaged through it quickly, finding what she thought she would need. She grabbed the small wooden box that held all of her essential oils. She also took her stethoscope, some bandages, and one of her medical books. She handed them to Daniel, who placed them in his saddlebags. Then Emily opened up a carpetbag and retrieved one of the dresses she had brought with her. She quickly pulled it over her blue jeans and T-shirt, then said, "Okay, I'm ready. Oh, wait! Tommy, would you mind staying here and looking after my things?" She said this while tapping the chest that held her money with her hand.

Tommy slowly nodded his head, finally recognizing what she meant.

"I'll take care of everything, Em'ly."

Daniel mounted up on Hoss, then asked Dolly, "How long

ago did David leave?"

Dolly said, "Only about fifteen minutes ago. You might catch him before they launch the ferry if you hurry."

Then Daniel noticed Hank's body still draped over the horse and asked, "Do you have room in the cemetery for this fellow?"

Dolly replied, "We'll take care of him. You get moving, now."

Emily untied the mare from the back of the wagon and quickly swung herself into the saddle. Then she and Daniel galloped down the trail heading for the Duck River, with the colt following behind.

As they reached the edge of the River, they saw that the ferry was nearing the opposite bank. Daniel tried to yell loud enough to get David's attention, but the river's rushing sound was too loud. He looked at Emily and asked, "Can you whistle to get their attention?"

Emily stuck her two pinky fingers in the edge of her mouth, one on each side, and let go with an ear-piercing whistle. David and Tom looked across the river and found Daniel waving to them. The two of them pulled against the ropes of the ferry to bring it to a halt. Once their momentum had ceased, they began to pull back to the nearby bank toward Daniel and Emily. When David came closer to Daniel, he yelled out, "Nafkl! You come back!"

Emily looked at Daniel and asked, "What did he call you?"

"Nafkl," said Daniel. "It means brother."

When the ferry raft reached the bank, David said, "Good you come back. Uncle very sick. Sarah say get Daniel."

Daniel said, "Well, I won't be much help, but this is Emily. She's my wife, and she is a medicine woman. She can help Chief William."

David looked at Emily and nodded, though Emily wasn't sure whether or not it was a nod of approval. They loaded the horses onto the ferry, and then Tom and David pulled against the ropes to move the ferry back across the Duck.

When they mounted their horses, David, Daniel, and Emily rode at a gallop for quite a while until the horses tired. They all knew how important it was to get back to Sheboss to give the chief the necessary medical care to regain his strength. The trip would take nearly a full day's ride at a normal pace. They were hoping to cut that in half. They walked their horses for about an hour, allowing them to slow their breathing down to a normal pace. Then, they mounted again and galloped down the trail for as long as possible.

They finally rode into the stand around noon. A small camp had been set up in the clearing, not far from the corral. As they rode up, Sarah came out of the cabin with a concerned look.

"Daniel!" she called out as they rode closer. "I was afraid you had already left us to go back home."

Daniel replied, "I was on my way when I met Emily on the trail. Sarah, this is my wife Emily."

Sarah nodded to Emily with a small smile. "Chief William isn't doing well at all. He's burning up with fever."

Emily asked, "Where is he?"

Sarah pointed toward the camp where eight teepees stood. Sarah said, "He's in the one closest to the trail. David will take you to him."

Emily dismounted from the mare and handed the reins to Daniel. She followed David to the camp, carrying her medical supplies with her.

David and Emily entered the teepee and found David's uncle lying on a mat. The chief's skin was beaded with droplets of sweat from head to toe. He was conscious, but only barely. Two other men were inside the teepee attending to the chief, but neither was knowledgeable about medical treatments. They were taking turns wiping the chief down with cool water, trying to bring down his body temperature.

Emily knelt next to the chief and felt his forehead. She reached into her bag and pulled out an old glass thermometer. Holding it in her hand, she looked up at David and asked, "Does he speak English?"

David replied, "He speak little English. Not as good as me."

Emily turned back to Chief William and said, "Please tell him I need him to place this under his tongue and hold it there. But don't bite it. Just hold it between his lips."

David did as she asked. Chief William opened his mouth, so Emily could place the thermometer under his tongue. While she waited for the thermometer to register, she took out a stethoscope and listened to his heart and lungs. His breathing was labored, but as far as she could tell, he didn't have pneumonia yet. When she checked the thermometer, it read 102 degrees. Emily turned back to the men attending to the chief and asked, "Has he been coughing or sneezing a lot?"

The men looked at David with confusion on their faces. David spoke to them in Chickasaw, asking them the same question Emily had just asked. They responded to him, and then David translated. "Yes."

Emily asked, "What else? Has he complained about pain?"

David again translated, and Emily watched as one of the men touched his head, then rubbed his hands down each arm and the length of his body. David then translated, "He say head hurt. All body hurt. Hurt start two days back."

Emily reached into her bag and pulled out a bar of soap. She tossed it to David and said, "Tell them that he has influenza. Tell them to heat some water, wash their hands with that soap and the hot water. Tell them not to touch their faces with their fingers or the palms of their hands. If their face itches, tell them to use the back of their hand to scratch. Understand?"

David translated to the men, then responded to her, "They understand."

"David, have you had contact with your uncle since he came here?"

David said, "No."

Emily instructed, "Tell them that anyone who has touched the chief in the last few days should do as I instructed them to do."

David translated again. The men nodded, then walked outside to bathe themselves.

"David, influenza is contagious, I mean, you can get sick too if you touch him. If you don't touch him or come too close to him while he coughs or sneezes, you should not get sick."

David nodded his understanding. Emily continued, "Can we build a fire in here?"

David nodded to her question. "Okay, let's get a fire built and I need a pot to boil some water in."

David left the teepee to find what Emily had requested.

Moments later, David brought in a bucket of water, an old tea kettle, and wood to build the fire. Emily filled the kettle with water and added eucalyptus, peppermint, lavender, tea tree, and lemon oils. She placed the kettle onto the fire to heat the water and bring it to a boil. She asked David to close the flap of the teepee so that most of the steam from the kettle would remain inside the teepee. There was an opening in the top of the teepee that would allow the wood smoke to escape so they wouldn't suffocate. Once the water began to boil, steam escaped the kettle's spout. The aroma of the oils filled the teepee. Emily moved the kettle so the spout was directed toward the chief. She encouraged him to take deep breaths. She had David bring in fresh drinking water and encouraged the chief to drink often to fight against dehydration.

Emily attended to the chief all afternoon and through the night. The next morning, she woke from dozing off while she sat next to the chief. He, too, was awake. He was alert and feeling better, although not yet ready to resume his normal place in life. Emily called for David and asked if he could get Sarah to prepare a broth for the chief to eat.

Chief William sat up to eat the broth, then lay back down, still too weak to move much. Emily continued to vaporize the inside of the teepee with the essential oils for the rest of the day. She made sure that Chief William drank plenty of water and ate small amounts of food. The next day, he was no longer coughing, and he could move around outside the teepee a little.

Emily had decided that he would be fine and that it would be safe for her to leave him with his people. She returned to the cabin and found Daniel sitting at the table in the dogtrot, drinking coffee and talking to Sarah. As she walked up, Daniel asked, "How is he?"

Emily responded, "He'll be fine. We caught it early enough."

Then Daniel asked, "Would you like some coffee?"

She replied, "I think I'd just like to get some sleep."

Daniel pointed to the door behind him and said, "Your bed is in there. Sleep as long as you like."

Emily slept for nearly ten hours. She woke to the aroma of some meat cooking. "*Chicken?*" she thought.

She rose from her bed and walked to the dresser, where a pan of water, soap, and a towel awaited her. She undressed and bathed herself, then put on fresh clothing. When she stepped out of the cabin, she found Daniel, Sarah, and David starting to gather around the table. Daniel walked over to Emily and hugged her, then asked, "Are you hungry?"

Emily replied, "I could eat a bear."

Sarah kidded and said, "Well, we had bear last night. Will you settle for chicken?"

They all chuckled as they sat down to eat the chicken, potatoes, and pinto beans Sarah had prepared.

The sun was beginning to set, just peering over the tops of the trees and beyond the clearing west of Sarah's stand. They ate their meal together and shared stories of the last six months. Daniel finally asked, "Emily, why did you come here? I was going home to meet you."

Emily replied, "I got a letter telling me I should come. It told me how to get here and that I should be prepared when I came."

Daniel asked, "Who sent you the letter?"

"I did," she replied.

Daniel looked at her suspiciously. Emily reached into her skirt pocket and pulled out the letter to show him. Daniel read the letter with a look of awe and wonder. He then handed it to Sarah so she could read it. Sarah read it aloud so that David could hear.

Daniel then asked, "But what will we do? We don't have a place to live. How will we make our living? Where will we live? What about our house back home? Your job? My job?"

Emily smiled at him, then said, "We're going to do what you always wanted to do back in Hampshire. We're going to live life simpler and live it to the fullest."

Daniel smiled at her and grabbed her to hold her in his arms.

David rose from the table without a word, then walked from the cabin toward the Chickasaw encampment. Emily looked at Sarah and asked, "Did we say something to upset him?"

Sarah replied, "No, David does things without warning all the time. He was never taught to excuse himself from the table."

The three of them watched as David entered his uncle's teepee. Then Emily turned back to Sarah and said, "Let me help you clear the table and do the dishes."

"No!" said Sarah. "I wouldn't think of it. You and Daniel take a walk while I do this. You haven't seen each other for a while. I'm sure you've got lots to talk about."

Daniel and Emily took a stroll around the stand, catching up on the news. Daniel shared his adventures at Grinder's Stand, including meeting Davy Crockett and the incident at Sheboss Stand with the men who attacked Sarah.

Emily told him about receiving the letter from her grandpa, the vault at the Davy Crockett Museum, all the gold and silver she found, and the guns and tools she brought. She told him about buying the mules and the wagon, learning to shoot, and selling most of their livestock. Then she told him what she did with the farm, how she deeded it over to Frank Lovell because he had helped her so much during the past six months.

Finally, Emily asked, "Where do we begin?"

Daniel replied, "Well, I think maybe we should go back to the Gordon place and talk to Dolly. She'll probably have some ideas about that. Besides, we've got to go back and get our gear."

"All right," said Emily. "Can we leave in the morning?"

Daniel said, "As early as possible."

Daniel rose early the next morning. He was too excited to sleep. All he could do was think about the new life he and Emily would build together in this new place. As the two of them exited the cabin, they met Sarah. She handed Daniel a poke containing food for their journey back up the Natchez Trail. They all said goodbye, and when Daniel and Emily started walking toward the corral to get their horses, David promptly met them. He was leading their mounts, all saddled and ready to go. Daniel shook David's hand and thanked him, then he and Emily mounted their horses and rode away.

Near the end of the day, they reached the ferry crossing. Tom stood at the far bank as they rode up. He waved, then started pulling the raft toward them. As he reached the river bank where they waited, Daniel said, "Hello, Tom. How are you?"

Tom replied, "I be jest fine."

Tom helped to load the animals onto the ferry, and then he and Daniel pulled on the ropes to start the raft back toward the Gordon place. Halfway across the river, a shot rang out. Then another and another. They were coming from the direction of Dolly's house.

"What is that?" asked Emily.

Daniel replied, "Gunshots, coming from Dolly's place."

He and Tom pulled against the ropes harder, trying to reach the opposite bank as quickly as possible. Once on the other side, Daniel checked his weapons to ensure they were all loaded with dry powder. He then looked at Emily and said, "Stay here."

"No way!" she yelled back at him. "I'm right behind you."

The two of them mounted their horses and rode toward the Gordon House, ready for whatever lay ahead. Tom followed on foot, carrying his own rifle.

Less than five minutes later, Daniel and Emily rode into the clearing where the house stood. Gunsmoke hovered over the field, making it difficult to see who was who. Painted men on horseback rode through the encampment, wielding weapons like tomahawks, bows, arrows, and lances. Projectiles darted through the air all around them as they dismounted to prepare for battle. Guns were being fired from the house and the corral as the painted men rode through randomly, firing their weapons.

Daniel found what he was looking for. Just twenty yards ahead were the tables where everyone shared their evening meals. He said, "Come on and stay low!"

He and Emily ran toward the tables. Daniel kicked one over when they reached them and ducked behind it, dragging Emily down with him. "Can you load?" he asked her.

"Yeah, but I can shoot too!"

Daniel said, "All right, take your first shot, then keep loading as I hand them to you. We've got four rifles and my two pistols, so keep 'em loaded for me."

Emily nodded her head with understanding. Daniel took off his bag containing his lead shot and powder horns and handed them to Emily.

"Here we go!" he yelled.

He and Emily were both fired at the same time. Daniel's shot was true and took down one of the braves as he rode past them. Emily's shot went wide. She had never attempted to hit a moving target in her practice sessions with Tommy. Daniel shoved his empty rifle at her, then took the next rifle and fired it. Emily quickly began loading the empty guns, trying to overcome her shaky hands as she did.

As the men rode past, Daniel noticed their faces painted red and white while their hands were painted black. The Black Hand! he realized. As Daniel raised his rifle to take his third shot, a brave wielding a tomahawk leaped from his horse and landed on Daniel. The two men rolled on the ground from the impact. Emily gasped as she watched the brave sitting on top of Daniel, his tomahawk raised, ready to split Daniel's head open. Daniel grabbed the brave's wrist, pushing against him to keep him from striking his blow. Having no fear for her safety, Emily rose from behind the table. She lifted the rifle high above her shoulders and swung it down, striking the brave in the back of the head. As he rolled away, he quickly landed on his feet and raised his tomahawk again. Emily lifted the rifle once again, pointed toward the brave, and squeezed the trigger. This time, her shot hit its mark. The brave fell backward, and he landed face-up on the ground. His eyes remained open, but he was dead.

CHAPTER 16

E mily stood over the brave, stunned by what she had done. Daniel jumped to his feet and tackled Emily to the ground, knocking the wind out of her. A brave rode past them screaming. He had missed his shot. His lance, which had been intended for Emily, harmlessly bounced off a rock that was peeking up out of the ground. Daniel grabbed Emily's hand and dragged her back behind the overturned table. Emily choked and coughed before finally gaining back her breath.

Suddenly, fifty warriors appeared from the trail that led to the Duck River. Daniel's heart dropped in his chest. How could they hold off an army so big, he thought. The black-handed braves all lifted their hands and screamed when they saw the warriors riding toward them. In unison, they turned their horses and rode away, leaving a trail of dust.

Daniel realized these warriors were not part of the Black Hand. These men were not painted. They had not ceremoniously prepared themselves for battle. It was Chief William Colbert and his travel party. They all rode into the camp with their horses dripping wet. Then Daniel noticed the riders all had wet legs. They had crossed the Duck River without the benefit of the ferry.

As the Black Hand fled, Chief William motioned for several men to pursue them. Twenty of the warriors rode off in pursuit. The chief rode up and stopped in front of Daniel and Emily and spoke to her in his native tongue. Daniel translated the chief's words for her.

"He asks if you are okay."

Emily instructed, "Tell him I am fine and thank him for coming to our rescue."

Daniel translated back to the chief. Then, the chief stepped down from his horse. He looked around and instructed his remaining braves to look after the wounded. When Emily realized what they were doing, she said, "Oh, Daniel! We need to help them."

She moved from body to body, checking for survivors and for those she could help medically. They carried all the injured to the house, which would be used as a temporary hospital. Titus Finley, Dolly's foreman, was one of the injured, along with Dolly's sons, Micah and James. Ten slaves had been killed. Eight women and two men.

After Emily had tended to the wounded, Chief William asked that she and Daniel sit with him to talk.

Daniel translated for Emily, saying, "He came here because he didn't have a chance to thank you for what you did in healing him. He wants to thank you now. His nephew David told him of our conversation last night, of how we would like to settle here. He wants us to stay. He wants to give us land to build our home. He wants to keep you close in case his people need a medicine woman."

Emily smiled as she replied, "Please tell him I will help his people in any way that I can. It will be my honor."

The chief spoke again, and Daniel translated: "He says there is land just east of here, a valley that sits next to the Duck River. He wants us to have it."

Then Daniel gasped as he said, "Emily, it's nearly 200 acres!"

Emily chuckled with excitement at the news and thanked the chief using the Chickasaw words that Daniel had taught her. Chief William told Daniel that he and his men would escort them to the property the next day. Daniel and Emily shook the chief's hand and continued expressing their overwhelming gratitude before leaving him.

That night, after supper, Daniel and Emily excused themselves so they could walk together to discuss their future.

"I can't believe this is really happening," Daniel said. "This is just all so surreal."

"I know," said Emily. "But isn't this just what you wanted? We're going to live simpler lives and live them to the fullest."

Daniel smiled and asked, "Did you finally drink the Kool-Aid?"

Emily laughed, saying, "I don't know about that, but I do know where you got that saying. I read your book while you were gone."

Daniel asked, "You did? Finally! Did you happen to bring my book with you? I love that book. It could come in handy here."

Emily looked up at him, seemingly baffled.

"Are you kidding?" she asked. "I couldn't bring that book with me."

"Well, why not?" he asked.

Emily, still baffled, responded, "Daniel, you grew up thinking you had something in common with the writer of that book other than the fact that you shared the same name. Don't you realize yet that you didn't share a name with this great writer of history? The reason I couldn't bring that book with me is you haven't written it yet."

ABOUT THE AUTHOR

 Michael L. Clark was born in Tacoma, Washington, but grew up mainly in the south. Over the years, he has worked as a farmhand, elephant handler, zookeeper, restaurant manager and owner, musician, cake artist, and rural mail carrier, all while honing his craft as a storyteller.

Clark's debut series was inspired by his many trips down the Natchez Trace. The stops along the Trail mentioned the people who once lived on the trail but gave limited information about their lives. Clark began to wonder about their stories and imagine traveling back in time to live among them and learn more. That desire sparked the idea for his first novel, The Shimmering, which has since evolved into a series of time-traveling Historical Novels.

His fourth novel, Ambush at Horse Creek, is the first of many books he calls The Young Americans series. Each story depicts a young person growing up in a historical situation. Ambush is about a teenage boy who rides for the Pony Express.

BOOKS

OTHER TITLES BY

MICHAEL L CLARK

The Diary of Gus Childers: The Shimmering Book 2
The Prophet: The Shimmering Book 3
Ambush at Horse Creek
The Red Raven: Book 1
Raven's Destiny: The Red Raven Book 2